MUSIC
of the
SPHERES

MUSIC
of the
SPHERES

MICHAEL BURKE

A Caravel Mystery
from Pleasure Boat Studio: A Literary Press
New York, NY

Music of the Spheres
© 2011 by Michael Burke

ISBN 978-1-929355-70-9

Design by Susan Ramundo
Cover by Laura Tolkow
Cover art by Gunilla Feigenbaum

Caravel Mystery Books is an imprint of Pleasure Boat Studio. We are a proud subscriber to the Green Press Initiative. This program encourages the use of 100% post-consumer recycled paper with environmentally friendly inks for all printing projects in an effort to reduce the book industry's economic and social impact. With the cooperation of our printing company, we are pleased to offer this book as a Green Press book.

Our books are available through the following:
SPD (Small Press Distribution) Tel. 800-869-7553, Fax 510-524-0852
Partners/West Tel. 425-227-8486, Fax 425-204-2448
Baker & Taylor Tel. 800-775-1100, Fax 800-775-7480
Ingram Tel. 615-793-5000, Fax 615-287-5429
Amazon.com and bn.com

and through
PLEASURE BOAT STUDIO: A LITERARY PRESS
www.pleasureboatstudio.com
201 West 89th Street
New York, NY 10024

Contact Jack Estes
Fax: 888-810-5308
Email: pleasboat@nyc.rr.com

1

IT WAS LATE SUNDAY night, it was pouring rain, and I was facing a "ROAD CLOSED—DETOUR" sign when LeRoy called me. I had just turned my second-hand twelve-year-old BMW coupe with the dented hood and rusted side panels on to Machinist's Drive. I drove by Iron Inc, the rusted remains of a once-thriving iron industry, passed by Pharm-a-Lot, the drug factory outlet that was one of the few industries still thriving, and headed down the last mile of unlighted road toward my home in The Gold Hill Arms. Heavy spring rains combined with the thaw of winter snow to give Hammer Creek the boost it needed to swamp the culvert, overflow the road, and carve a three-foot-deep ditch into the gravel. I pulled up to the edge and stopped. A couple of million years and I would be sitting on the rim of an eastern Grand Canyon. I didn't have the time, or maybe I did. That's when Wagner's Valkeries galloped through my cell phone.

It was LeRoy.

LeRoy is not the kind of guy who would call anyone very often, especially on Sunday, especially after ten o'clock at night. He runs a bar in the center of town and for some reason or other I had spent quite a bit of my life there. He was a good bartender who knew when to talk, when to listen, and when to just keep quiet.

"Blue?" That's my name, or at least that's what my friends call me. "You remember Billy Windsore?"

I remembered Bill. He wasn't the nicest guy I knew, but he hung out at LeRoy's and I shared drinks with him now and then. About twelve years ago his father, George Windsore—everyone called him Mister George—was stabbed in the back as he lay in bed. You couldn't help but feel a bit sorry for Bill.

"And you remember Hank Menotti?"

Sure do. Hank was a pathetic character, the bastard son who turned up out of nowhere. He pleaded guilty to stabbing Mister Windsore, got sent away for manslaughter, and was serving time in the state pen.

"Well, he's back," LeRoy continued, "and he was here tonight."

Out of jail already? That was quick, and why did he come back here?

"I'm worried," LeRoy said. "Any chance you could go by and check on Bill?"

"Why me, LeRoy? Why not the cops?"

"Look, this is pretty vague and I don't like dealing with those guys anyway. The whole thing is just a hunch, and if they did run across Hank, you know they'd beat the shit out of him and try to throw him back in jail. They didn't like him twelve years ago and they won't like him now."

LeRoy was right. LeRoy was always right. Maybe bartenders are always right because when you sober up in the morning you realize that you were wrong. "Okay, LeRoy. Maybe I can cancel a couple of appointments and drive over."

"Thanks, Blue. One on the house next time you come in."

I backed to the edge of the road, turned the Beamer around, and returned to the highway. I welcomed a good reason not to go back to my empty apartment. Bill lived by the reservoir; three miles along Route 25, ten more on Route 131, then a left on to South Reservoir Road at the light after the Three Bears Bistro, a 24-hour eatery on the edge of town. It attracted drivers on the way to work, coming home from work, and those who didn't work at all. Food was cheap, parking free in back, and you could sit in a booth there as long as you wanted. The rich folks living down South Reservoir Road didn't stop there. Their maids, nannies, and gardeners did. By the time I reached the Bistro, the rain had stopped and a mist had settled over the road. Cars on the street would materialize out of the white fog and disappear just as quickly behind me. I could just make out the traffic light ahead. It was red. I'd been around this town long enough to know that one could beat the light by cutting through the parking lot behind the Bistro. I turned at the Three Bears sign and started around the back. The driver of the black car coming toward me turned on his headlights at the last second and all I could see were two white balls of light. A quick swerve to the side and we passed, but I nicked the bumper of a shiny blue something-or-other parked behind the Bistro. The black sedan that blinded me kept going, scattering gravel as he turned onto 131, leaving me only with a fuzzy image of the balding top of a short driver's head. Something told me I'd better not waste time here and I kept on.

Bill's house was the first on the left, one of a row of vacation homes looking over the reservoir, each separated from its neighbor by unfriendly high hedges. It was an area where the rich used to escape from the city, but now it had been absorbed into the suburban fringes. I turned off the engine and let my Beamer coast down to the end of the driveway and stop in front of the garage. A new white Mercedes peered at me from under a half-closed garage door, watched me get out and start across the gravel to the house. It was old-fashioned modern; two story, flat roof, windows that reached from floor to ceiling, and a deck that wrapped around from front to the back where one could sit and look out over the water. On both sides of the house a lawn stretched out, trimmed like the buzz cut on a new recruit. The peony bushes at the far edge were isolated in a brown mulch, and not a weed was in sight—the work of a gardening crew from south of the border. Heavy rains had soaked the pregnant buds on the stalks, bending their heads to the ground. The front of the house was dark. I rang the buzzer, then knocked, and knocked again. I pounded on the door but there was no response.

I followed the deck to the side of the house, the squishing of my shoes making a sneak entry impossible. The fog had laid a white blanket over the reservoir. A light from a back window sent a ghostly glow over the water. I peered in through the glass and could see an empty easy chair, a broken glass lying on the rug, and a book opened face down on the floor. The body that lay face down next to it was nude from the waist up. I tried the back door; it wasn't locked and swung open. The red drooling gash in his back grinned at me. I rolled Bill over. He looked up at me with a glimpse of recognition.

"*Blue*," he gasped, then, "*Red . . . Green . . . Red . . . Yellow . . . Green.*"

"Billy! What the fuck happened?"

Bill looked toward the ceiling with dying eyes and spoke so softly I had to lean close to hear him. "*Red . . . Green . . . Yellow . . . Yellow . . .*"

"Red what? Hold on, I'll get help."

"*Red . . . Greeee . . . .*" Bill's head dropped to the side. His eyes rolled back and he was gone.

LeRoy was right again. He knew something was up. He was one of those guys who operate just on the edge of the law, guys who are experts at knowing when that edge is about to be crossed. I sat on the steps that led from the deck down toward a pier. The fog had lifted, the moon had risen and left silver streaks across the water. A frog took a dive by the shore, and concentric circles moved slowly outward, rocking the moonlight. A full police crew was inside. Inspectors, crime scene experts, a photographer, and some guy who specialized in outlining dead bodies with fluorescent yellow tape. A couple of neighbors walked along the path by the reservoir, staring, wondering what the fuss was about. I followed them along a trail that wound through a thick grove of prickly barberry bushes. The trail curved upwards, through a forest of maples that shut out any trace of the sky, and opened on to the parking lot behind the Three Bears Bistro. A few cars were parked there; the black sedan was long gone. I looked for the clean blue car that I nicked—it wasn't there. The Bistro faced the highway; no one sitting in the booths would have seen anything that went on in the parking lot in back. The couple turned the corner ahead of me. I followed them around front and into the Bistro, took a seat at the counter, and ordered a coffee and a piece of coconut custard pie to calm my nerves. A portly woman in a well-oiled apron took the order and returned with the goods. Before I could ask a question she asked me what happened at the Windsore house. News travels quickly. The couple who had preceded me up the trail were sitting at the other end of the counter. They stopped talking to listen for my response. I said it wasn't good, that Bill Windsore, the guy who lived down by the reservoir, was dead. They pressed for details and by the time I left they had dragged quite a bit of information from me, and I got nothing in return. I left out the part about the colors.

2

WHEN DEATH LOOKS YOU in the eye he challenges you to look back. He dares you to fall back on the normal excuses to try and ignore him. Just try telling him about reincarnation, rebirth, heaven, the afterlife, alternate universes, universal consciousness, religion, infinity, eternity, insanity. He forces me into the present, into the boredom of logical life, to focus on every detail. How I place the key into the ignition, start the car, turn the wheel to pass the Bistro, look at it, pretending it is the same as it was when I passed it a couple of hours ago. I perform: I steer, I dim my brights for an oncoming car, I'm nice to someone I will never know.

I turn on to Machinist's Drive. The washout forces me to take the long way around to get to the Arms. I drive past a few well-mannered houses, and then the tar ends and the gravel begins. The Drive tops a small rise and drops down to a one-lane bridge. Tonight Hammer Creek, a usually quiet and friendly stream, churns below. The foaming water forms a silver snake in the moonlight. I drive over the bridge and past a field that once produced corn, then through a stretch of forest that forms a tunnel over the road. I haven't come this way for a while, but the mood hasn't changed much. Nothing changes much on Machinist's Drive. The locals call it Hobo Alley, compliments of the railroad yards, but a number of years ago it was upgraded to Machinist's Drive. I call it Factory Road. That seems to fit it best, although most of the factories have shut down or are running at half speed. I drive past the dark shells of the abandoned Warren Furniture Company and the equally deserted Warren Storage Company and see the glow of Apollo Lighting up ahead. Apollo Lighting is a business in decline, down from its heyday about ten years ago, but it casts a luminous halo over the landscape, seducing drivers into believing they are protected. In front of the factory stand rows of orange trucks with tired pneumatic lifts resting on their backs, piles of light poles, huge coils of wire shaped into pyramids, and a small mountain of discarded traffic lights. The factory itself is undistinguished, a two-story cinder-block windowless structure a block long, but it brags of self-importance by covering the grounds with a glaring light. Spotlights are mounted on the edge of the roof and on a series of poles in the yards, lighting not only the factory but also the surroundings and the sky. Until tonight, Billy Windsore was owner and president of Apollo Lighting and that proved to be a disaster. The business was built up by Bill's father, Mister George, and it was one of the few factories on the Drive that thrived. After his father was killed, Bill took over. For the past decade the factory had been in decline, and rumor had it that it is close to bankruptcy. Past Apollo Lighting and before reaching the Arms lies a large graveyard filled with marble mausoleums and monuments. Bill's father, Mister George, is buried in the grandest of the mausoleums. Down the hill toward the back the graves are marked by smaller cheap headstones with names that have been eroded by the wind and rain of time, or not marked at all. The classes keep to themselves, even in the afterlife. Apollo's glow keeps the north end, the rich end, under a permanent shine twenty-four hours a day. Light is tough on ghosts. The lower-class area over the edge of the hill is far from the light. The bodies in those graves get the best deal—they are in the dark and can come out at night and play.

The Gold Hill Arms is on the south side of the cemetery—four stories, brick, unassuming. Its history parallels the rise and fall of industries. Now not many workers stay there. The top floor has been condemned and remains empty. I live on the third floor. The place has become the home for society's misfits, prostitutes, and loners who would like not to face questions about their life. I see Sylvia enter—Sylvia, who lives down the hall from me and usually remains invisible. She doesn't see me. I park my car in the usual spot next to the panel truck that has been sinking into a muddy grave for years and walk up the few steps to the front door. The lobby is a large space, hinting at some long-lost glamour. Javier, who lives in a ground-floor apartment, keeps a couple of flowerpots going on both sides of the entrance. Javier runs the place, but no one seems to know who actually owns the Arms. Javier has been there for years, but there is no sign of him tonight. Sylvia is ahead of me and walks wearily toward the stairs. Young, pretty, thirties maybe, not married—I wonder why. I check the mail and grab a copy of the free Factory Focus so I can fill the rest of the evening reading the ads for day care, psychics, and septic tank cleaning services. I follow Sylvia.

I can't imagine why she would move into the Arms. Cheap housing I guess, or she wants to be anonymous. She is carrying a take-out pizza and three books that she holds tightly against her chest, an armor plate of protection. She runs the local library. The library is open for the normal daytime hours, but Sylvia keeps late hours. She is too deep in thought to notice me. She is slim, not tall; a young and pretty librarian. She has dark brown hair held tightly in place by a wide plastic clip. I follow her up the stairs at a distance that keeps my eyes on a level with her bottom. Her dress, a smooth blue silk, slides over her as she moves up the steps. I keep my pace in sync with the alternating oscillation of the slippery material. She reaches the third floor before noticing me. A quick "Hello Blue" and her key is in the lock of 3A.

"How's the library doing?" I asked quickly, before she can disappear.

She stops. "Fine, Blue, fine. Thank you."

"Are you going to eat that pizza all by yourself?" I ask, trying to keep the conversation alive.

"I'll save what I can't eat for tomorrow's lunch." She closes the door behind her and I'm left standing alone, looking through the wall into her apartment. She tosses the books and pizza on to the couch. She unsnaps the plastic hair clip letting a cascade of brown curls fall over her shoulders. She reaches around to the back of her neck, takes hold of the zipper and pulls it down to her waist. The dress slides gracefully to the floor, where it forms a puddle of blue at her feet. She is wearing nothing underneath, unbefitting a librarian, and turns toward me. Her breasts are small and intelligent; her soft stomach curves to a enticing dimple of a belly button, and below, a finely woven . . .

"Is there anything wrong?" The door has opened and Sylvia is looking at me with a puzzled expression. She is still holding the books and the pizza.

"No. Just dreaming a bit. It's late . . . ."

"Yes it is. Goodnight, Blue." She closes the door.

Down the hall no light shines under the door of 3B. Stella works the strip club at LeRoy's; she won't be home until after three in the morning. I slide the key into the lock and open the door to 3C—the place I call home—click on the overhead and look around. I am disappointed to see everything in its usual place. I am not sure what I expected to see, I am not sure what I wanted to see, and I am not sure whether I want to be there at all. But my easy chair looks friendly so I hang my coat on the back of the door, kick off my shoes, and settle into the maternal comfort of the cushions. I start to nod off when a steady drum beat begins pulsing through the wall from 3D. Eddie is home, as usual. His radio blaring, as usual. And by now he has drunk himself into a stupor, as usual. I know from experience that knocking on his door is a futile gesture, but we'd worked out a system without ever acknowledging it. The fire escape runs the length of the building and his window is never locked. I climb out my window and into Eddie's apartment to turn down the radio. He is crumpled into a lounge chair, oblivious to the world, an empty bottle of whiskey and a glass on the floor beside him. No one knows much about Eddie. He is using booze to wipe out his memory's hard drive, and he isn't sharing secrets with anyone except Jack Daniels. I helped him carry the chair he was sitting in from the street when he moved in a couple of years ago. We didn't talk then and not much since. Back through the window to my place, mission accomplished, all's quiet. He will never say anything about it, and neither will I.

My chair faces away from the wall—a mirror image of Eddie's. I make myself a martini, turn the chair, rest my feet on the window ledge and gaze out the window to the west over the railroad yards. The ground drops sharply at the back of the Arms over an overgrown expanse of barberry bushes. Beyond and stretching into the distance are the old Erie and Lackawanna railroad yards. They are not used much now, but every so often an engine pushes a group of freight cars along a track, parking some, separating out a few for a long journey to somewhere. The boxcars closest to the bottom of the hill haven't been moved for years, and seeds grow from between the rails and the rusted iron wheels. There's no activity tonight, a quiet night, a quiet that is ancient and timeless, a quiet that carries a music of its own. A music that floats noiselessly over the rails, over the past, over my thoughts. It's a tune that's been around for a long time—Pythagorus heard it first. Well, he didn't actually hear it, he felt it, and he figured out the source. The Music of the Spheres, a harmony, musical notes of frequencies created by the rotation of the planets. No orbits in those days, the planets rested in spheres around the earth. They rotated at different speeds, created vibrations in the ether, musical notes. Transparent spheres, crystal I like to think, and they make a beautiful sound. The chime of two glasses of fine crystal, filled with aged wine, touched together in a toast to friends. It is an unheard harmony that quiets the nerves of the universe, quiets my nerves.

Time to mix another martini. My formula: gin, two drops of vermouth, a twist of lemon, and lots of ice. The ice is important. The first taste wakes up the palate, then, as the ice melts, the martini gets weaker and weaker but the taste persists. The first sip of the next martini surprises with the same wallop as the first. It's a method designed to keep the continued consumption of martinis pleasurable. It fits my life style. Mixed the third and settled back in my chair. The rain has stopped, the clouds have moved on, and the three-quarter moon casts its colorless light over the tracks. The air is heavy with water, still chilled by the remnants of a tough winter. A quiet night in April. My sign, Taurus, is hanging over a distant mountain, stubborn and lonely. The twins are due next, Gemini, but they are too faint to be seen tonight. They straddle spring and summer, leaving a split personality. Maybe that's where the good-twin/bad-twin idea comes from. Soon they will take their place in the sky, but tonight the nearly full moon rules and leaves the stars struggling for attention.

Sylvia really is pretty, in a high IQ kind of way, with a lovely figure and quiet brown eyes framed by all-too-present librarian's glasses; hair clipped into a tight dark-brown bun with a few strands fighting to get loose. Sylvia, the name fits her. Sylph: a slender woman of light and graceful carriage. Reserved, shy maybe, but not too friendly. Perhaps she is just unfriendly to me, an idea I don't want to dwell on; so I think about Bill instead. Brought to a lonely end in his lakefront house, watched over by an expensive white Mercedes. He was never married and had no heirs; his only relative was his brother Jason. He was a difficult guy to make friends with, and I think he relied on Leroy's Bar and Strip Club for companionship. More than once we sat at the end of the bar and talked about nothing over drinks. What was he trying to say? *Red . . . Green . . . Red . . . Yellow.* It was as though he was hypnotized and stabbed to death by an alien. Mars has risen now over the railroad yard and glows red on the horizon. I fall asleep in the chair, thinking about flying saucers soaring silently by on their way home, flashing red and yellow lights around a silver disc.

3

THE POLICE HEADQUARTERS—a five-story brick building on the corner of the town square—had been given a face lift. The bricks were re-pointed, the marble lintels cleaned, and a new chrome-and-glass revolving door surrounded by translucent panels replaced the original entrance. The old worn building was threatening, but it was honest. The new makeover fooled you into believing that you would come out the same as you were when you went in. The force used to throw some jobs in my direction whenever they needed an undercover guy, or something done that would embarrass the department if they were caught in the act. Most of the crew who had put up with me back then had moved on. Kathy McGregor left for the capital two years ago when she landed a sweet position in the Governor's security detail, but JJ was still around. Inspector, now Captain, JJ Cakes had moved up in the world, up from the third to the fourth floor. His office now had a window that revealed a sliver of the park.

I greeted him. "Pretty snazzy, JJ. What did you do to deserve this?"

"Easy. Just stayed around long enough while everyone else got promoted to bigger jobs in bigger towns. Sit down, Blue, haven't seen you for a while. How are things? How's life? How are the martinis?"

JJ had grown a bit rounder, a bit balder, and was wrapped in a coat and tie that fit him ten years ago. He was not a large or intimidating guy, and the small-time thugs he would bring in tended to get sassy with him. That was their mistake. The surface of his desk was still piled as high as I remembered, with a mixture of files, reports, papers, and family photographs of the wife and kids.

"So, Blue"—JJ got right to the point—"Officer Corbutt tells me that you were the first to find Billy Windsore last night. What were you doing there?"

"LeRoy, from the bar, called me and asked me to go by. He saw Hank Menotti in town, out of prison, and he could sense trouble coming on."

JJ frowned. "Last time he was here, about twelve years ago if I remember right, it was bloody. You and me, Blue, we were the first ones there."

It was a grisly crime that I hadn't forgotten. Now I get to be the lucky guy who finds the son, stabbed in the back just like his father.

JJ turned back from the window. "So the guy gets out of prison, full of hate, and comes back to settle some scores. So why didn't LeRoy call me?"

"LeRoy runs a bar and strip joint. He knows to stay clear of the men in blue."

JJ took out a pad and began searching for a pen. I saw a ballpoint sticking out of a pile on my side of the desk—pulled it out and handed it to him. "Been looking for that," JJ said to himself. "Now, let's go over this. You told Corbutt that the back door was unlocked. Bill was stabbed just before you arrived, maybe you scared the murderer off before he could finalize the job. You didn't see anybody. So far that's it for clues, except for his last words. 'Red, green, red, yellow, green!' What the fuck?"

"Obviously a flying saucer landed in the back yard, did a bit of that *Close Encounters of the Third Kind* music-and-lights stuff, slid out a ramp so a little green alien guy with big eyes could come in and use his tentacles to carve up Bill's back. Case closed."

"Glad to see your detective skills haven't left you, Blue." JJ hesitated, then reverted back to the efficient lawman. "Look, we need to find out what LeRoy knows. I know he isn't going to open up to the police, but you've known him for a while. Maybe you could follow up. Tell you what, I'll put you on a retainer. I haven't done that for a while, but it used to work. You saved us a couple of times. Find out what you can from LeRoy. Is that good with you?"

"Getting paid to hang out in a bar, now that's my idea of a good job."

"Good. Pick up a temporary ID at the front desk; you might need it. I'll call down. And Blue, it's good to see you. If you ever want a full-time job here, we might be able to figure out something for you to do."

"No thanks. I'm addicted to sleeping in. The private-eye business has been a bit slow but it usually picks up when the weather gets warmer." *Non-existent* would have been a better word than *slow*. I did have a tough case last month, tracking down that guy's lost lawnmower. I solved it. He'd left the motor running and it wandered across the street into his neighbor's garage.

JJ shifted uneasily in his chair. He had some news, but wasn't sure how to break it. "By the way, you know that Kathy's back?"

"No. Why would she come back here? That's a nice gig she's got with the Governor."

"Maybe she misses you. It's been two years."

It was a nice thought. I didn't say anything.

"Anyway, she came back to replace Chief Jones upstairs."

"Chief Katherine McGregor." For a moment I let myself believe that Kathy had come back to see me, but promotion to Chief of our Police Department was incentive enough.

JJ shrugged. "It's a nice promotion for her. But you gotta admit she does deserve it. Her beauty fakes people out, but remember when she karate-chopped that mafia dude who went for her gun?"

"Who could forget?" The picture was fresh in my mind. "And she could outshoot the whole department on the target range." I chuckled. Kathy was a good choice for Chief. "Well, JJ, that means Kathy's your new boss?" I said without thinking.

JJ didn't answer, and I didn't press it. Kathy used to work for him and now she was coming back as his supervisor. Might make a guy worry what garbage can the last twenty years of his career had just dropped into.

"You're working for us now, remember, Officer Johnny Heron." JJ reminded me.

"So?"

"So guess who else Kathy is now the boss of." JJ grinned. He was running some scenarios through his mind. The grin grew. "Now, let's imagine you guys, you know, are kinda in bed together, and you need a raise." JJ started to giggle.

"Okay, Captain, and she says there's no position open at the moment."

We left each other sporting teenage grins, trying to cover up a lot of history neither of us wanted to think about.

4

THE MURDER OF MISTER George Windsore wasn't easy to forget. A warm August evening about twelve years ago, and JJ and I were driving back from upstate. His family had escaped the hot summer sun of our town and they had taken me along for a weekend to force some fresh air into my lungs. Private eye jobs were scarce, I was daydreaming my life away, and JJ had figured that a walk in the woods would have a positive effect. But the weekend was over, and he was driving me back to my easy chair and himself back to his desk for a week of police work, leaving his wife and two youngsters to enjoy the country. I was planning ahead on spending time on the fire escape, sitting in the plastic chair with my feet on the rail, martini in hand, watching over the railroad yards and the sky. I could watch the trains come and go by day and watch the stars come and go by night.

JJ drove and the night descended and we talked and traded police stories and private eye stories, married stories and unmarried stories. As we drove, the fields began to fill with single-family homes, the houses grew closer together, then became low-scale apartments, which gave way to strip development, then shopping malls, offices, and apartment buildings. JJ, always on duty, had his police radio on when the 911 call was patched through. Some hysterical guy called in crying about his father. He didn't make much sense, but somebody was dead, and the nearest car better get over to check it out. We knew the address, Merrimac Road, on the edge of the state forest. JJ radioed the dispatcher that we were only a few miles away and would follow up.

Ten minutes later automatic sensors turned on lights to mark our progress down the long smooth driveway of the Windsore estate. George Windsore and his wife Mary had lived here. Their sons were grown and had moved out. Mr. Windsor's position in the town called for a certain respect, but his nickname 'Mister George' also came from the cold distance one felt in his presence. Mary had died of a nasty cancer about a year before and now Mister George stayed home alone. By day he kept himself busy running Apollo Lighting. He advertised by filling his property with lights: lights in the trees, blinking lights around the house, lights along the porch steps, and spotlights to light everything else. He had a virtual monopoly on contracts for the city: street lights, traffic lights, stadium lights, and enough billboard lighting to keep our residents from getting too romantic about the stars. I wondered if Mister George was afraid of the dark.

The house began its life as a beautiful old Victorian mansion with a sharply peaked roof, gable windows, and some rare ornamental woodwork along the eaves. Mister George bought the house and a stack of acres and paid for it all with our tax dollars. The old Victorian was still there, but he was in the process of strangling it with expensive additions. A three-car garage was attached to the right side, a couple of faux Roman pillars framed a new porch on the front, and a glass addition grew out of the bottom floor like a giant carbuncle. The three cars in the garage all looked brand new—washed, waxed, polished and expensive. An out-of-place rusted Chevy pick up was parked in the driveway. We pulled the cruiser up behind it.

Although the grounds were lit like an amusement park, the house was dark, except for one light that glimmered from an upstairs window. We stood on the porch and listened. The place was strangely quiet. JJ reached for the doorbell, but just as he pressed it car lights swung down the driveway. We turned to watch a shiny MGB convertible slide to a stop behind the cruiser and a well-dressed young guy jump out. That was the first time I'd seen Billy Windsore.

"What's wrong? Any trouble, officer?" He was puzled to see a police cruiser parked in his father's driveway.

JJ responded in his best police voice. "Answering a call. Who are you?"

"Bill Windsore. This is my parents' house."

The door of the Victorian flew open. A distraught figure stood there, pale and shaking. Bill shouted at him, "What the hell are you doing here?"

"He's up there, he's . . . dead. Oh my God." The ashen-faced figure pointed a bloody finger toward the second floor.

JJ pushed him aside and we ran into a dark cavernous living room. A stairway rose dimly along the far wall leading to the second floor. We charged up the stairs, Bill running behind us. It was easy to tell where to go. A shaft of light shone from an partly open doorway, lighting a trail of bloody footprints along the hallway. JJ pulled out his pistol and moved ahead slowly. He pushed open the door to the master bedroom. We were looking at a Halloween stage set: a chair on its side; a fallen bookshelf, books scattered over a bloodstained carpet. Bed covers and sheets were pulled to the floor and half-covered the bloody form of a man. He was wearing loose pajama bottoms and nothing on top. He lay on the floor face down. His bare back was criss-crossed with cuts. Blood was oozing from the gashes and a red stain surrounded him on the carpet. A cry, a scream shattered the air. Bill, who had followed us into the room, fell to his knees in a pool of blood, pulled his lifeless father to his chest, and began to sob.

We found the guy who met us, the guy who called for help, slumped in the front seat of the rusted pickup, his head lying against the steering wheel. That was Henry Menotti, the abandoned bastard son. Yes, I remembered the Windsore murder.

5

I PARKED THE BMW BEHIND LeRoy's Bar. An alley sloped down along the side of LeRoy's Bar leading from Main Street to a parking lot in the back.. The lot was used during the day by city employees, and at night by the patrons of LeRoy's who preferred to park anonymously. I left the Beamer squeezed uncomfortably between two fat SUVs, and walked up the alley. LeRoy's was located just off the town square, a half block from the police station, which didn't please our town's guardians of morality. LeRoy's hid behind a dark wooden door marked with a small hand-lettered sign; LEROY'S BAR. The sign had stayed the same for years until recently, when LeRoy converted the basement to a strip joint. Now a bigger sign was added above the entrance proclaiming, in flashing blue neon: 'LIVE GIRLS.' LeRoy was getting fancy; LEROY'S BAR AND STRIP CLUB.

I looked forward to the abrupt change from the midday sun to the perpetual night at LeRoy's. I could settle directly into the night, bypassing the sentimentality of evenings, avoiding the metaphysical shudders brought on by the ending of the day, the closing of hopes brought by the setting sun, the sunset, the slow awakening of the streetlights and the quiet that slid over downtown sidewalks. Daylight wasn't welcome at LeRoy's. The only windows to the outside looked over the alley. One in LeRoy's office, one in the men's room, and one in the women's room if my memory served me correctly. The décor hadn't changed in the last fifteen years. The long room had a bar running the full length of one side backed by a grand mirror. A handful of tables was scattered randomly around the space; their position changed with the tastes of the patrons. A few were lined up in more orderly fashion against the opposite wall. An alcove opening off the main room allowed couples to find a table where they could meet and drink with a bit of privacy. LeRoy must have been thinking of an English pub when he hung a dartboard on the wall by the front door. Entering customers would have had a good chance of losing an eye if all the darts hadn't been lost years ago. The bar itself was a magnificent relic sporting a rich surface of dark mahogany. Cushioned stools with shiny silver legs were lined up in front, and the brass foot rail, probably more valuable than my retirement IRA, stretched along its length. The entrance to the downstairs Strip Club was through a door to the right of the bar. A hand-lettered sign by the stairs advertised the goods:

TONIGHT

See *CARMEN* ride the Pole
Let *DeeDee* lift your spirits

And featuring
STELLA STARLIGHT
Dancing to the
MUSIC OF THE SPHERES
(no cameras allowed)

Behind the bar was an impressive array of liquor bottles with exotic labels that could lead an alcoholic to believe he was studying the history of brewing. LeRoy knew that it didn't help business if the drinkers could see reflections of themselves, so he had covered the mirror with autographed photographs of near-famous customers, once-funny cartoons, and fire and building permits. At 10:30 in the morning the place was nearly empty. The guy sitting at a table had apparently started early or perhaps was left there from the night before. A large bearded fellow with long white hair was behind the bar. That was LeRoy. He was diligently polishing away the doldrums that remained on the brown mahogany when he saw me come in. "Good day, Blue. Sorry to bother you last night—guess I jumped to conclusions. Sit down, I do have some coffee back here."

I sat on a stool and took the coffee. "Billy Windsore was a steady customer here."

"Yeah, I'm fine. Sure the business is good. I'm in good health. What else was it that you wanted to know?"

"Sorry. I'm not very good with the pleasantries."

"He often dropped by after work. Came for the booze, but mostly he came for the strippers. I think he was in love with Carmen, one of my dancers." He pointed to the sign. "You know him. He was one of the regulars."

"I like martinis. He liked scotch. We talked. I kinda liked him, or maybe felt sorry for him."

"Or maybe you identified with him," LeRoy added. "He kept his life private—you know—a bit of a loner."

I agreed, LeRoy had a point. "When there's something in the past to forget you find someone else who's hiding. And then you share not talking about it."

LeRoy sympathized. "I know. Anything to escape. There was something in his brain that he needed to subdue, a fire burning inside him that he needed to extinguish, a hunger that had to be fed, a thirst that must be quenched." LeRoy was waxing poetic. "He was drowning it in expensive scotch and sex. But then I guess we all have our demons."

"My demons don't understand me," I grumbled under my breath.

LeRoy didn't hear me and went on, "Did you go by? How's Bill?"

I looked down at my coffee. "Sorry LeRoy. Your intuition was too good. He's dead."

LeRoy stopped polishing and stared at me.

"Last night," I continued. "After you called I went by Bill's place. It was late and nobody answered the bell. I saw him through the window, on the floor. Stabbed in the back."

"Stabbed?" LeRoy repeated.

"It must have happened just before I arrived. I got there a few minutes too late. He faded out in front of me."

LeRoy's expression didn't change. I knew he was upset , but he wasn't the kind of guy who would show it. "He wasn't everybody's idea of a decent guy," LeRoy said thoughtfully. "But it's still a shame. Did Hank do it?"

"I don't know. What happened here last night that made you worry?"

LeRoy glanced at the figure at the corner table who was concentrating on his midday beer and decided he was too far gone to eavesdrop. "Bill was here, drinking, having his usual Glenfiddich on the rocks. He left for a few minutes, went downstairs and returned with Carmen. The place was filling up, a noisy crowd. Bill and Carmen took a table in the far corner of the alcove. Over there." He pointed. "Bill had an open tab, and every so often I'd send the waiter back with another scotch for him and a seltzer for Carmen." LeRoy looked over toward the table. "Damn, stabbed in the back. Damn!"

"Was Hank around somewhere?" I asked.

"That's a bit later. He comes up from downstairs with Stella on his arm. It's not the first time he's been here—been around a couple of times this week. Usually sits at the end of the bar and nurses a beer. Doesn't talk much—he doesn't really know anybody here. Prison changed him some. He looks a lot older. He was just a kid when they put him away; in his thirties now. His hair is long, in a ponytail, and he's lost a lot of weight. You can see he was a good-looking guy but now he's pale—haggard, really. Not much joy in his face. I don't know what's going on between him and Stella, Stella Starlight. She lives near you, right?" LeRoy waited for an answer.

"She's right down the hall. Just on the other side of my living room wall. Keeps me up whenever she brings home a paying customer."

LeRoy nodded sympathetically. "Business is business. I guess she's good at what she does, but it's just business."

"What are you driving at?"

"Well, I can't tell whether she prefers boys or girls. She certainly wows the guys, but there is a pretty steady girlfriend. She often waits out back in the car to pick Stella up after her last dance. Stella is a strange gal, almost like she's two different people."

"So what's the connection with Hank? Business?"

"I don't think that's business. There's something between them, although it seems a bit explosive." LeRoy was interrupted by a couple who entered the bar looking for an alcoholic breakfast. He filled two drafts, carried them over, came back, and picked up the tale of last night's drama. "Anyway, all's fine for a while until Bill gets up to leave. He walks by Hank's table and their eyes meet. Hank jumps up and says something. I couldn't hear what, but the crowd began to back away. Carmen looked over at me and motioned for me to come over. I was pushing my way through when Hank leaps at Bill and grabs his throat. Tries to strangle him on the spot. Took me and a couple of customers to pull them apart. We held Hank back, and Bill left the place as fast as he could. Didn't say anything to anybody—left Carmen standing there."

"Did you find out what Hank said?" I asked.

LeRoy frowned. "Versions differ, but essentially it was 'you mother-fucking miserable slimy piece of shit,' or something in that vein."

"I get the point. What happened after Bill left?"

"Hank quieted down, took his seat at the table with Stella. They were talking and the place returned to normal, whatever that is at night in a bar full of drunks and misfits. My crowd is used to fights—doesn't dampen their enthusiasm. But then after a bit I saw Hank hand something to Stella and she gets up and heads for the door. I don't know. Something he said to Stella must have riled her. That's not an easy thing to do—she's as hard as nails. Stella stomps out. Hank sits for a couple of minutes, then jumps up and races out after her. He looked pretty upset."

I was trying to make sense of the soap opera. "When did you call me?"

"I should've called you then, but the place was busy and it wasn't until about an hour later that I got to thinking about it. Hank hated Bill and Bill's brother Jason and cursed them to hell when he was sent to prison. That doesn't seem to have softened over time. I began thinking about Hank attacking Bill. That's when I called you. Should've called sooner. Should've, could've—story of my life." LeRoy wiped his brow with the dish towel and then threw it down the bar in disgust.

"Don't beat yourself up, LeRoy. You didn't have much to go on." I watched the dismayed bartender retrieve his towel. "Maybe I'll drop back later and talk with the dancers when they come in."

"Tomorrow, Blue. They're off Mondays. See you then." I started for the door when LeRoy called out after me. "You're parked out back—you can go out downstairs through the back door of the Club. It's unlocked."

I left Leroy staring at the pictures behind the bar. Murders have a way of focusing the mind on stuff you've avoided for a long time. The door leading down to the Club was open. I went in, past the empty ticket booth, through the second door and down the stairs. The Strip Club was deserted. The only light was from a few dim red bulbs. Chairs were turned upside down on the tables. Reminders of last night—cigarette butts, crumpled paper napkins, and a few empty beer bottles—were scattered on the floor. Without a throng of eager gazers to hold it back, the red velvet wall paper was threatening to wrinkle itself off the walls. The round stage in the center, with a quartet of silver poles, looked like a lonely carousel waiting for the horses to return. The air was heavy, weighed down by the noises of the night before. I walked across the room and pushed open the back door. The sunlight was blinding. It reminded me of the different world that lay outside. The walls of LeRoy's divided the two worlds. Outside, the clockwork world lit by the midday sun; inside, the timeless underworld of sex and booze and shadow.

The confrontation between Hank and Bill left me with a lot of unanswered questions. I had to find out more about the original Windsore murder case, and there was still time enough in the day to get to the library. The Beamer was waiting for me. A turn of the key brought the engine to life with a burst of enthusiasm. Main Street was quiet. The light at the end of the alley was red, but there were no cars coming from either direction, so I ignored it. The rear tires squealed, and it didn't take long to get my 280 horses up to the speed limit.

On the way to the library, I drove a couple of blocks off Main Street in order to pass by Rick Jones Used Cars—a gas station surrounded by a sea of cars. Rick had lined up a row of highly polished SUV's along the front. A large sign advertized the best deal—only $159; per week, per month, a down payment, you decide. The cheapos were parked on the side of the lot, and they looked the part. Dents, rust spots, a blue door on a black Chevy. An aging Ford pick up that was trying to put on a good face. A Chrysler limosine with tinted windows that probably still had a body in the trunk. And next to that, my old Honda. I had felt a tinge og guilt when I left him there, but he did decide to quit on me. In a rainstorm at 2 in the morning, on a deserted road, 50 miles from town. What do you want? I think he winked a headlight at me as I drove by, just to say 'no bad feelings.' I gave him a tip of my virtual hat and turned back towards Main Street.

The Library was about ten blocks away, by the elementary school. Sylvia was the librarian.

6

THE PARKING LOT FOR the George Windsore Public Library was packed. The congestion was caused not by a sudden interest in reading, but by the press conference the Mayor was holding in the upstairs meeting rooms. I left my car parked behind a dumpster and wove my way through rows of cars to the two sets of glass doors at the entrance to the building. A small sign advertised the hours. A temporary sign standing beside the right-hand doors advertised the press conference that was taking place in the George Windsore Conference Center upstairs. I remembered reading about proposed changes to the zoning, better described as a rewrite of the blue laws, another attempt to limit what the town thought was sexual deviation by changing the laws to freeze out the bad guys. It won't work; sex is a human version of Whack-A-Mole. You knock it down in one place and it will come popping up somewhere else. You might as well try to ban hard-ons.

Officer Corbutt and a cop I didn't recognize stood stiffly by the entrance, posing as security guards. Their real function was traffic control. Corbutt was the first cop who answered my call on the night Billy Windsore was stabbed. I nodded to him. He nodded back.

Corbutt shrugged his broad shoulders. "So Blue, what do you think?"

"About what?" Corbutt made me feel small. He was a big guy with ripped muscles that tested the strength of the stitches in his uniform. When he shrugged his shoulders he looked like he was lifting barbells at the gym.

"You know. You told me. 'Red, green. Red, yellow, green.' Sounds like the Windsore guy was killed by a traffic light." He laughed, and his buddy laughed too.

"So your crew came up empty-handed?"

"We checked with the neighbors. They're not close by, and the only one who saw anything was a grandpa sitting on his porch opposite the entrance to the Windsore driveway. He remembered seeing an old wreck of a BMW drive in, but nothing else."

I looked up at Corbutt, "What do you mean 'old wreck'? A couple of rust spots and a dent . . . ?"

He grinned, "Sorry, Blue. Didn't mean to insult your love. We figure that whoever bumped Bill off must've parked behind the Three Bears Bistro and walked over. There's a path along the water that's pretty well hidden from sight. But nobody at the diner could help us either." He was interrupted by two reporters, late for the conference. Corbutt took his time checking their IDs, and then sent them in. "So why are you here, Blue? Worried they're going to shut down your favorite bars?"

"I'm here for the library."

"Dang, Blue. You're full of surprises."

I left Corbutt and his buddy chuckling to each other and stepped inside. A short hall turned the corner and opened onto a grand space built at a time when a collection of books gave credibility to our claims of being a civilized race. The reading room rose to a gold-leafed ornate ceiling thirty feet above. Rows of heavy wooden tables filled the space, each flanked by solid chairs and topped with evenly spaced shaded lamps. Four elegant chandeliers hung at the level of the balcony that ran along three sides of the room. Two spiral cast-iron staircases bracketed the balcony. Every wall was covered with shelves; every inch of shelf was filled with books obediently standing side by side, begrudgingly supporting the latecomers who lay sideways on top. A gap on each wall between the shelves promised passageways lined with ancient texts stretching into eternity. Sunlight streamed through tall vertical windows that opened the upper reaches of the far wall to the sky. Everything was made of polished brown hardwood: wood floor, wood chairs, thick wood tables, wood shelves, and books made from trees. Sylvia sat at a desk facing the rows of tables; she presided over the estate like a benevolent dictator. The rest of the room was empty except for a guy in the back who needed a place to sleep. The teen-agers wouldn't get here until after three, when school was out.

I remembered how the library served as a refuge for me when I was in high school. I'd slump down in a chair and peer at Barbara Jane Headly over the top of an assigned book and imagine walking with her into the stacks and getting lost deeper and deeper in rows of books and finding a good book, *Story of the Eye,* to read together, sitting side by side on the floor, our backs against dusty volumes of forgotten fiction, and I would have to explain, no, demonstrate the part with the egg, and Barbara Jane would giggle, then lift her short cheerleader's skirt and . . . .

"Good afternoon, Mr. Heron. What can we do for you today?" Sylvia greeted me formally, but warmly. She was more comfortable on her own turf than in an empty hallway at night dealing with a lecherous neighbor.

I avoided a number of suggestions that sprang to mind and stayed on the subject. "Remember the Windsore murder, some time back? I need to learn more about it."

"Your best source, maybe your only source, would be the newspapers." Sylvia fell into efficient librarian mode. "Can you tell me anything else?"

"The whole case from beginning to end was only a few weeks. That was about twelve years ago, around this time of the year."

"Take a seat at one of the viewers over there by the reference shelves; I'll get you set up." Sylvia could lead you to a rare out-of-print novel without even checking the catalogue. She knew of reference books that specialized in arcane information, books which hadn't been opened in years. I think she knew the location of every book in the library by heart. One seldom got the pleasure of browsing, as she would send you to a seat and return with the requested book and a couple of others that you hadn't realized you wanted until they appeared. She brought me a series of microfilm reels that recorded the newspaper articles of the time.

I spent the next two hours staring into a screen, digging through the gory details of the infamous murder. Then I looked through pages on the trial—there wasn't much of an actual trial, so the newspapers had to concentrate on rumor. The city had Hank dead to rights—scene of the crime, motive, blood on his hands. The prosecutor, a Thurmond Peck, let him plead guilty to manslaughter for a twenty-year term instead of murder in the first degree, which would have put him away for life. The papers weren't too interested in the legal details. Peck came off looking like a strong and no-nonsense guy, good for the community and good for Peck's election campaign. He was running for District Attorney. Hank Menotti went to jail. Peck won the election.

I was getting bored with the case, and my mind wandered to Sylvia. She was concentrating on her work, writing notes at her desk. The librarian at my high school was left-handed; Sylvia was left-handed. I wondered if librarians, like surgeons, were mostly left-handed. I wondered if anybody had ever written a thesis that matched left-handedness with particular sexual preferences. I think all policemen are right-handed. It sounds like there's a theory here somewhere. I was trying to think of anything but the case at hand in order to take my mind off a middle-aged guy lying naked in a pool of blood, his skin slashed to ribbons. I forced myself to concentrate on the task and went back to the newspaper records. Most of the press were positively gleeful over such a good scandal. They'd just finished with a front-page story of a preacher, child porn, and molestation. The police had searched the computer of a Reverend Jones and found a pile of dirty pictures. By the time the courts realized that there were no kids involved and the computer search was unconstitutional—the porn was legal, the search was not—the press had screamed with moral indignation and the poor guy's life was ruined. His preference wasn't for kids—he obsessed on older, tall, gray-haired women wearing black garter belts and stockings and tennis sneakers. Tennis sneakers, no less! The story was getting stale and the press was eager for a new scandal, so the murders mercifully pushed him off the front page.

One feisty paper, *The Alternate View*, was livelier to read, as the editors had been gunning for Windsore for years, and they wrote as if they thought he deserved to be murdered. *The View* went after him for ripping off the taxpayers. Apollo Lighting was making tons of money from the city, paid for by city taxes, and many of the contracts appeared to be awarded without the formalities of competitive bidding. Their main gripe was that Mister George was a tightwad and gave nothing back to the city. *The View* was pretty snide about it all and ran a series of editorials questioning his contracts. Then they ran a couple of stories about two incidents where Billy ended up in the hospital. One was a fall down the stairs and the other some kind of skateboarding accident. *The View* hinted at foul play but stayed vague enough to avoid getting sued. Nothing came of it, just accidents, and Mrs. Windsore backed her husband's account. A year before he was killed, the bad publicity threatened to put a damper on his business, so Mister George decided that he had a great interest in philanthropy. After Mary Windsore died, he got serious and gave a bunch of money to the library and conference center, which they gratefully named for him: The George Windsore Public Library and The George Windsore Conference Center.

I decided I had learned enough about the Windsore case when the teen-agers began arriving at the library, amid much chatter and flirtation, mostly modern updates of the old impress-a-girl-by-dropping-a-frog-down-her-dress style that was popular when I was young. I stopped by Sylvia's desk on the way out. She was writing diligently and didn't look up. I stood and watched her fingers push the pencil across the page, watched the red nails flash as though sending a secret code. The pen stopped suddenly when she realized I was standing there.

"Mr. Heron. Did you get everything you need?"

"Yes, you steered me in the right direction. I was able to get a pretty good picture of the case."

Sylvia accepted the compliment with a nod of the head, and then asked, "Why are you so interested in the Windsore murder case? That was a long time ago."

"The son was murdered just Sunday night—too late to make the papers."

She did not seem surprised. "Do they know who did it?"

"Not yet. There's one prime suspect."

She looked down and began sorting through papers on her desk. "Who would that be?"

"Can't say—I'm officially Officer Heron now. Sworn to secrecy."

"So the case is pretty much closed?"

"No. I didn't say that. Why the interest?"

"Oh. Just curious I guess. Let me know if you need more information."

"Okay. Thanks."

Sylvia had already moved on and her red nails were shuffling through library cards. "Any time, Blue, I mean, Officer Heron. We try to be helpful."

7

I WAS ENJOYING LYING IN the sun and watching the bikinis on a golden beach when my cell phone vibrated itself across the table and woke me when it hit the floor. I grabbed it before it could scurry under the bed, pried it open, and grunted something into it. In return, an official voice challenged me. "Is this Mr. John Heron?"

"Who's this? What day is this?" I sat up and searched for my watch. Eight-thirty. Who gets up this early?

"First Lieutenant Tom Flint. First precinct. My boss Chief McGregor would like to meet with you."

"Kathy?"

"Chief McGregor is free at nine-thirty this morning. The address is Seven Main . . . ."

"I know the address. I can be there at eleven?" I thought a shave and a shower would be a good idea before seeing Kathy.

"The Chief is free at nine-thirty, Mr. Heron. We'll see you then." A click signaled that the conversation was over.

I folded the phone closed. Have to go meet my new boss. Lovely Kathy—now Chief McGregor. Hadn't seen her for about two years since she got promoted to the state. We were so close, or were we? I never knew. Only a couple of phone calls since then; the distance was too much for either of us to deal with. Nine-thirty, I'd better hurry. I don't want to face the wrath of the new Chief. I found yesterday's unfinished cup of coffee languishing in the microwave and settled into the easy chair.

"Mr. Heron, it's ten-fifteen. They're inside waiting for you." Thomas Flint scolded me from behind his nameplate at the reception desk. A proud, fresh-faced young fellow, brimming with self-importance and sporting a uniform that had arrived heavily starched from the cleaners about ten minutes ago. I smiled down at him and pushed the door open into Chief McGregor's top floor office. Windows on two sides brought in more sun than I was used to in the Police Department. JJ had sunk into an office chair to wait, and Kathy sat on the side of her desk. I remembered the soft brown hair, the wide blue eyes with a tinge of green, and the long legs. They were crossed and a touch of thigh showed above a skirt that seemed a bit too short for the Chief of Police.

"You're late, John. We are all busy." Kathy didn't look my way.

I turned to check which window was letting in the cold draft. They were both closed. I took a chair, JJ sat up straighter, and Kathy slid behind the desk that Chief Jones had left behind.

She started in without any preliminaries, "Tell me, John, just why did you show up at Windsore's place Sunday night."

Coming from Kathy, the 'John' sounded strange, but I also tried to maintain a professional role. "LeRoy, from the bar, called me and said he was worried about Bill Windsore. Apparently Hank . . . ."

"Who's Hank?" Kathy interrupted.

JJ leaned forward in his chair and filled in the background. "Some years ago a son who was abandoned by Mister George, that's George Windsore, turned up out of nowhere and murdered him. A strange case. No one knew Mister George had a bastard child, and as far as I can tell they never saw each other before that night. That was Hank, Henry Menotti. He was sentenced to twenty years for manslaughter. He was a model prisoner, served the minimum and was released from prison about a week ago. A parole officer over in Tungsten was assigned to him. Hank checked in with him and is living in an apartment over there, but we sent a guy over and couldn't find him. I've posted an undercover cop outside the place."

I took it from there, "LeRoy said that Bill and Hank got into a fight. He knew Hank's history and was afraid he might go after Bill. LeRoy called me and I went to Bill's place to check on him. Got there too late. That's about it."

"That's not much to go on," said Kathy, still looking at JJ. She hadn't looked directly at me since I arrived. "Tell me more about the murder of the father."

I thought I could impress my new Chief with my research. "I spent the day in the public library yesterday."

"Library? Really?" Kathy's eyes met mine for the first time.

I smiled at her. Yes, Kathy's back! I thought. I'd missed her more than I wanted to admit.

"That's where that pretty librarian works, isn't it?" Kathy teased.

"Well, somebody has to turn my pages."

JJ was getting impatient. "Will you two cut it out."

A fierce stare from Kathy silenced him, and I continued. "The case was a front-page sensation. Some terrific headlines. *The Journal*: ABANDONED SON RETURNS— FATHER MURDERED or in *The Herald*: BLOODY HOMECOMING."

We were interrupted by the buzzing of Kathy's intercom. She listened briefly to Flint. "Excuse me a minute, guys. I have to talk with the DA." She pressed the button and answered very formally, "Chief McGregor here."

JJ stared at the floor while Kathy stared at her desk and listened on the phone and I stared at her. Memories were rising to the surface, memories so well hidden that I'd forgotten they existed. I dropped my eyes to her breasts and remembered the way they would nudge against my chest when she rolled on top of me. I remembered how she would let them touch my arm as she turned to use the computer and how I could peer between them as she bent over the papers on her desk, and how they peered back at me. In the morning she would dress up to the waist and leave her breasts bare as we stood and gazed out my window over the railroad yards. I would stand behind her and slide my hands down her smooth back, around her waist, up to her breasts, and roll her nipples between my fingers. But today she had them bound in snugly. Perhaps last night they had gotten out of hand and today she had grounded them with a tight, unforgiving bra. Police regulation uniform bra. Keep everything under control.

"Blue. Are you with us?" Kathy was looking at me, finally using the familiar 'Blue.'

"Just admiring your new badge, Chief."

"I'm not wearing a badge." Kathy brushed a strand of hair from her forehead. "That was the DA, Thurmond Peck. I may have told him too much. He wants to see you as soon as we're done here." Kathy was looking straight at me now with those blue-green eyes that always made me forget my next sentence.

"I suppose I could." I tried to be casual.

"It wasn't a request, it was an order." Chief McGregor was speaking now. "You were saying?"

"NAKED TYCOON MURDERED IN BED. That was the *Daily Flyer*. There was a lot of sensational press. *The Alternate View* headlined: HI DAD, I'M HOME! The trial was cut short. The prosecutor . . . ."

"Was that Peck?" Kathy interrupted again.

"Yes, and he was running for election to be District Attorney. He coaxed a plea bargain out of Hank and changed the charge from first-degree murder to manslaughter. Peck wrapped up the case about two days before the vote. He won the election, but it was a tight race and he obviously wanted to get a conviction into the papers to back up his image as a tough prosecutor. Also if the case had dragged on a lot of dirt might have come out. George Windsore wasn't the most popular guy in town; there were some pretty ugly rumors floating around about his contracts and even worse stories about his treatment of the kids."

"Anything solid?" Kathy pressed.

I shrugged, "No, all rumor."

"What contracts are we talking about?" Kathy asked.

"He ran Apollo Lighting. Now Bill, the oldest, runs it, or did until Sunday night. Jason, the younger brother worked there too, but didn't do much. He wasn't the brightest bulb in the factory."

JJ followed up. "All I know is that Apollo has contracts for most of our street lighting and all the traffic signals, stadium lighting, billboards, and who knows what else. Windsore contributed a lot to Peck's campaign for DA. He probably wanted to keep the law on his side. I doubt that Peck would have been anxious to see nasty stuff come out about a major donor. He got the case out of the way clean and fast."

"What about the brother, Jason?" Kathy asked.

"Nobody knows what happened to him," JJ chipped in. "Last heard from a couple of years ago."

"Wait," Kathy interrupted. "Let me get this straight. Mr. George Windsore has an affair with somebody. He cuts out and a child, Hank, was born. Then, twenty years later, Hank turns up out of nowhere and kills his father, who he never saw before. He gets convicted, goes to jail. Now he gets out of jail, has a fight with Bill at the bar, and then follows him home and stabs him to death."

"Maybe." I said.

"Maybe?" Kathy waited.

"Nothing solid. I just don't like it. A hunch, I guess."

"Another one of your hunches," Kathy sighed, remembering something.

JJ chuckled, started to speak, and then thought better of it.

"Okay," Kathy was wrapping up the meeting. "Keep after the Menotti guy; we need to bring him in. Anything else?" She was looking at me.

"One thing," I added. "There's a photographer, Annabel Lente. Most of the pictures I found in the papers, of the crime, the suspects, and the funeral, were taken by her. I think she works for you guys now. Mind if I talk with her?"

"Now she runs the Traffic Division," JJ said. "You can find her in their office in the sub-basement. I think they put them down there to keep the speeders who got tickets from finding them and getting revenge."

"I'll drop by." I figured the meeting was over, and got up to leave.

"You have an appointment with DA Peck," Kathy reminded me. "I'm coming with you. You've got time to check with Lente. I'll meet you out in front in forty-five minutes; I suspect you could use some official back-up." Kathy smiled at me and erased the last two lonely years from my memory.

8

A SECRET LABYRINTH WAS HIDDEN under the Police Precinct. The elevator dropped as far as the first basement and after that you were on your own. Each underground floor contained different levels, often requiring you to climb up stairs to go down, and each floor used a different numbering system. I walked from Level B-1 to B-2, but then found myself on sub-level B-1A. Down the hall and a few steps up put me at Level FF. A kindly maintenance man found me wandering aimlessly about and led me through the maze. I felt as though I was following Alice's white rabbit down the rabbit hole. Down some more stairs, along a hall, past workshops and storage rooms. After the next turn in the hallway, frosted glass doors advertised their contents: 'Special Data,' 'Evidence Storage,' and 'Guilt Assessment Services' (No admittance without proper ID). Some more intriguing doors were given initials 'BBD' and 'SL & R Control.' A few steps down and we landed in front of 'Traffic Division.' I thanked the maintenance guy. I should have asked him to keep the meter running and show me out in ten minutes.

The Traffic Division occupied a converted boiler room filled with files, a long table and chairs, and computer screens. Three twenty-year-olds sat in front of monitors that simultaneously changed to a new program when I entered. I asked for Annabel Lente and was introduced to a tall, handsome, thin woman with gray hair and rimless glasses. Miss Lente presided over the techno-geeks at the computers like a kindly mother hen. She knew the language: "Now Stuart, to access the previous record go to the arrest ticket link, click the jail bar icon, scroll to the first two digits of the account number, then enter the plate number and year." She left out the first step which should have been 'but first save your position in Grand Theft Auto.'

She turned to me. "How can I help you?"

"You used to be the police photographer? And I think you covered the Windsore murder case some years back."

"Yes. I haven't thought about that one for a while. How did you know?"

"A couple of crime photos appeared in the press. You were credited."

Annabel laughed, "Well it's nice to get some recognition. I used to be their official photographer, but now I manage the Traffic Division. Photography is more fun—certainly more interesting than sending out traffic tickets." Miss Lente reminded me of my English teacher in Central High. I had a crush on her. Whenever she smiled at me my daydreams would hide her grammar lesson in a warm fuzzy cloud. "As for the photos, I probably have the originals of anything that got to the press, but I can't give information to civilians. Who do you represent?" Annabel was good at her job—open, friendly, but not one to be pushed around. "The Police Department." JJ had foreseen this when he put me back on the payroll. "I'm Officer Heron for the moment, if that helps." I flashed my new ID card.

She looked at the card, then said, "Got that yesterday, did you? Are you reopening the case? Has something new come up?"

"Mister Windsore's son Bill was killed Sunday night and I'm looking into it. There might be something about the father's murder twelve years ago that could shed some light on the case, or it could amount to nothing at all."

"Now Bill Windsore is murdered." Miss Lente shook her head. "My God, that family certainly has had its share of misery. The murder of Mister Windsore was so awful that it was difficult take pictures—he was stabbed so many times. I had to step back, be an uninvolved observer. Looking through a lens has a way of distancing tragedy."

I understood the observer idea. It was a concept that saw me through a number of ordeals. "Are those pictures still around?"

"Yes, you're in luck. The old crime files are all packed away in our storeroom. They'll be here," she said with a certain pride. "Those old ones, the real photos, I can find them. What gets lost is the new digital stuff. Not really lost, just buried somewhere in an outdated computer file. Do you want real photographs?" she asked. "Come this way." Miss Lente led me into a small room off to the side. "This used to be my darkroom, my workshop, my home away from home, but now it's used for film storage," she said sadly.

The darkroom was filled with floor-to-ceiling filing cabinets that took form as my eyes got used to the dim light. Some of the cabinets were supported by the old developing sinks. Pale light from the one fluorescent bulb in the ceiling over the small table and chair made the room look like an interrogation chamber. It was apparent that no one spent much time here. "The files are in chronological order," Miss Lente said, gesturing to the wall. "These are the earliest. What were the dates?" I told her and she pointed to a couple of drawers. "Start here. I'm afraid I can't help. I'll have to leave you to find what you can. We have two new techies here and I have to get them started, but feel free to dig through." She left me facing the files—files stuffed with a photographic history of crimes, misdemeanors, and guilty faces.

I opened a drawer, rummaged around, and found the right year. The folders were in order but packed so tightly it was difficult to pull one out. I coaxed out two. The first was the file on the Windsore crime. It was packed with pictures; pictures of the Victorian house, the bedroom, and a number of difficult-to-look-at photos of the murdered man, in full-color detail. I understood why Miss Lente wanted to keep the camera between herself and the scenes. Deeper in the file I found some photographs of a guy being pushed into the back of a police van. I had to look closely to recognize Hank. His face was bruised and swollen and one eye was nearly closed. There were a lot of pictures of the Windsores, the estate, the sons when they were little, and the Apollo

Lighting factory. I found Bill in a number of photos, but the only picture I could find of his brother Jason was when he was about ten.

The second file was from the same time, labeled Reverend Jones, the priest I'd read about in the library. I took out a folder and was roaming through some images that the Reverend found titillating when Miss Lente came back into the darkroom. She closed the door behind her, then, never taking her eyes off me, she pulled her dress up over her head and dropped in onto a filing cabinet. I recognized the bra and panties; they were in a sexy ad that I had seen just last week. She reached around to the back and unsnapped the brassiere, letting it fall to the floor. She stepped out of her panties. She was looking into my eyes. I was looking at firm breasts, a small waist, and a soft black triangle set off by a black garter belt, silk stockings, and a large pair of New Balance blue-and-white breathable mesh model 560 rubber-soled cross trainers. I tried to concentrate on the mystical area framed by the garters, but the dammed sneakers kept getting in the way. Maybe Adidas would have worked, or Converse, or Puma, or . . .

I found a file on the funeral. A lot of people had shown up. Mister George was not well liked, but he had influence enough to convince the political crowd to take the day off. Our Mayor was there, some city council members, judges, and lawyers. I spotted a young version of Thurmond Peck. One color photograph in particular interested me. It was taken from a distance and included the entire audience. I took it out, left a marker in its place as instructed, and carried it out to the computer room to show to Annabel

Lente. She was helping a young guy at a console. I waited for her to finish and then asked her if I could get a copy of the photo.

She took the picture and looked it over. "Doesn't look too interesting to me but if you want a copy, that's fine, as long as I keep the original." She took the picture to a copy machine and returned with a color duplicate.

I thanked Annabel. She asked me to give her credit if I used the photo and to let her know if she could be of further help. The elegant lady escorted me to the door of the Traffic Division, gave me a warm smile, closed the door and left me standing in the hallway. I looked around for an exit sign. I should have left a trail of crumbs.

9

I MET KATHY ON THE front steps of the precinct. I was on time. We followed the edge of the park to the courthouse. Rain threatened from the west, but the sun still persisted and glistened off the soft brown hair that constantly fell over her eyes. Two years had only made her more beautiful. Nearly my height, she moved like a dancer. Walking beside Kathy brought back a forgotten sense of well being.

"Have you met our District Attorney?" Kathy asked as we cut across the corner of the park.

"Kathy, you have the most beautiful hair."

"He has a reputation for toughness, and he doesn't like anybody crossing him."

"When the wind blows, a most sensuous ear peeks out, with opening pedals like a spring crocus."

"For some reason Peck's not happy about you digging around in this case."

"Your eyes, Kathy, they are hypnotic, alluring, secretive."

"I suggest you tell him what he wants to know and stay away from snarky comments. I know that will be hard for you."

"And your lips . . ."

Kathy opened the courthouse side door leading to the offices and waved her arm before me. "After you, Romeo."

We passed through three different checkpoints on the way to the District Attorney's official suite on the third floor. Inside the office, the blond Playboy bunny who was posing as the DA's receptionist cheerfully welcomed us, then had us sit and read gun magazines to kill time while the DA kept us waiting, just because he could. In contrast with the blonde, the reception hall was large, bleak, and designed to intimidate—but it was the weasely cop standing next to the inner office door who made me nervous. He looked like an insect that had just crawled out of a mulch heap. His crew cut was short enough to allow the spots and blemishes on his head to peer through. His thin lips started on the left in a smile and ended on the right with a down-turned sneer. He had his hands stuffed deeply into the pockets of the uniform, giving the impression he was trying to find his dick. Even with his arms by his side, sweat stains darkened the blue around his armpits.

I whispered to Kathy. "Who the fuck is that?"

She leaned toward me. "Officer Weaver, the DA's bodyguard. More like the DA's private police force. He's kept around to scare suspects into admitting things, whether they did them or not."

I was watching Officer Weevil. He looked familiar. Weevil was watching me. "Looks like a bug someone should step on," I offered under my breath.

"Don't let his size fool you," Kathy warned. "Weaver and the driver are quite a pair."

"The driver?"

Kathy tilted her head toward a figure who had followed us down the hall and now stood in the entrance. He was the opposite of Weevil. A soft, round bear. He looked like he wanted a hug. "The driver," Kathy whispered. "Officer Kozimov."

"Kozimov. An apple dumpling," I suggested.

Kathy kept her voice low. "You don't want to meet those two in the dark."

A buzzer alerted the secretary and she nodded to Weevil. He opened the door and stepped aside, and was about to follow us in when Kathy stared him down and pulled the door shut behind us.

Nice, I thought.

DA Peck's office resembled a court room, with the man himself seated behind a desk large enough to accommodate a ménage-a-trois on the surface. He was tall, wiry, and imposing, a man who could look down on you from a sitting position. A long face hosted a thin bone of a nose, streaked gray hair, and small coal-black eyes that he aimed at us like a weapon. His jaw was locked like a clamped vise. A wide straight mustache was pasted on his upper lip. Maybe he would smile at an execution, but he certainly wasn't going to smile at us. He gestured for us to sit and I looked for the defendant's chair.

"Miss McGregor, why are you here? I asked to see Heron," were DA Peck's first words.

I was about to lecture him on the use of Chief rather than Miss, but remembered Kathy's advice to lay off the wise-ass stuff. Kathy ignored the slight and answered professionally, "I'm interested in this case, Mr. Peck. There's a lot of history here that seems to be unresolved, and I am Chief of Police now."

Peck frowned at the thought. "Fine, Miss McGregor, but I don't want things to be confused by outsiders messing around where they don't belong." He looked at me. "Mr. Heron, I think it would be best if you left this for the police department to handle. When we catch the culprit we will call you to testify about the death as you were apparently the first one there. We'll bring in the Menotti guy; that shouldn't be hard."

Peck's regal stance as he lectured me was betrayed by the motion of his mustache. The edges waved up and down as his upper lip moved as if it were about to fly away to find a more hospitable face to sit on. I couldn't keep quiet. "Sounds like you've already held the trial. There's not a shred of concrete evidence to link Hank Menotti with the murder. A quarrel between two guys in a bar isn't much to go on."

"Don't lecture me, Heron. If he's innocent, he'll get a trial," Peck shot back, leaving out the 'fair' part. "I know right from wrong."

"Do you? Moral certainty is a wonderful thing, isn't it?"

Peck glared at me.

"Moral certainty, the greatest force for evil ever invented."

Peck's bullet eyes narrowed, giving me a look that he usually reserved for the criminally insane. "Just stay out of this, Heron. Leave it to us to pick him up."

Kathy stepped in. "Actually, Mr. Peck, we've put Blue, I mean, Mr. Heron, on the payroll as a temp. We've done that before and he's helped us out. This time we feel that he has some personal knowledge of the case that will come in handy."

The DA scowled. He obviously didn't like the idea. "You do what you think is best, Miss McGregor. But if he screws things up, it'll be on your shoulders."

Kathy said nothing, and Peck decided to end the meeting. "Keep me up to date on everything that comes up, and that doesn't mean a week later or even a day later. Officer Weaver will show you out."

We left on our own accord, although I slowed down a bit in the outer office just to annoy the Weevil. He followed us all the way to the building entrance and watched as we walked toward the park. Walking on the sidewalk outside felt like release from prison. I tried to lighten the mood. "So, *Miss* McGregor, where do you think DA Pecker gets his public relations skills?"

Kathy laughed, so I asked her if she wanted to drop by LeRoy's for a drink.

"Blue, it's two o'clock in the afternoon. There are some rules in the Police Department—maybe I should get you a handbook."

"Okay. But thanks for sticking up for me in there." I kissed Kathy on the cheek.

"I have a feeling the handbook has a rule against that, too," Kathy sighed without conviction. " But the punishment is pretty mild."

"Like what? A spanking?"

Kathy smiled, "Well, maybe."

I watched Chief McGregor walk up the front steps to the precinct building, watched her push the revolving door and disappear inside. The door swallowed people like a Venus fly trap. I found a familiar bench in the park, sat down, stretched out my legs, leaned back and watched the door, hoping it might keep turning and send Kathy back out. Spring was threatening and I had no idea where to go next on this case. No leads to follow, not even a stakeout to waste time on. Waiting on the bench seemed like a good plan.

10

I SAT IN THE PARK for about a half hour before the revolving front door of the Police Station sent Kathy out. She came directly across the street and sat down beside me. We sat without speaking, watching the pigeons watching us. Kathy opened her bag and dug out the remains of her lunch. She scattered crumbs for the eager birds. I was jealous—to find ultimate happiness when someone throws you a crumb. It was an envious talent.

Kathy broke the silence. "There's a stripper named Carmen. As far as we know she was the last one to talk with Billy Windsore before he died. I just talked to her on the phone but didn't get very far. I'm sure she has something to say, but she's afraid of the police."

"Any idea what?" I asked, staying on the subject this time.

Kathy didn't answer right away. "No. I couldn't get her to loosen up. She's panicked. I could hear it in her voice." Then she turned to me and said, "Blue, people trust you. I don't know why but, dammit, they do. Maybe it's because you trust them. You'd let a child molester go free if he didn't charge you for baby-sitting. I think LeRoy told her you could be trusted."

I knew better than to doubt Kathy's perception. "I'll talk to her if you want. When and where?"

"I made you an appointment with her. Tomorrow, about six p.m. at the diner. She'll be there."

"You think I spend my waking hours at the strip club, but actually I've never seen Carmen, on or off the poles. How do I recognize her?"

"That shouldn't be too hard. A six-foot blonde with breasts the size of watermelons. I think you'll pick her out of the diner crowd."

"How do you know that, about the watermelons? I didn't know you hung out with pole dancers."

"I went out with the bouncer a few times. He introduced me," Kathy said off-handedly. She had a way of giving me information I didn't want to know.

"You wouldn't know her full name or have any background info?"

"No, but I'll look into it. LeRoy has to have something written down, although I wouldn't vouch for the accuracy. I'll look her up, and the other dancers too while I'm at it." Kathy got up to leave.

"Kathy, how did you know I'd still be here, sitting on this park bench, watching the pigeons?"

"Looked out the window—you hadn't moved."

I didn't want to let her go. "Wait. One more question. Do you love me?"

Kathy looked down at me. "Of course I do, Blue. But two years apart is a long time."

"Then could you see moving in with me?"

"What? Moving in to the Dung Hill Arms. Home of the deadbeats! And what? We could raise a family and have hookers for baby sitters and pushers to read the kids bedtime stories. Are you kidding? Not a chance. How about you, Blue, could you get a job? I mean a real job, maybe earn some steady money?"

"Get a job? Nine-to-five? And then what? Go to church on Sundays, join the Rotary Club? Who do you think I am? But you mentioned babies. Want to have a few?"

"Babies! Have you ever looked around the police precinct? I have enough babies to take care of—certainly don't need any more."

"Think about it. A little Kathy with brown hair and a sundress. A little Blue, with short pants and a crew cut."

"A crew cut?" Kathy started to giggle. She took one step toward the street but then turned back and asked me, "Blue, do you think we could ever agree on anything?"

"Kathy, do you want to sleep with me?"

"Of course I do, Blue." She looked me in the eye. "I guess we were made for each other. Your place or mine?"

"You're right about my place. A prostitute through one wall and a noisy drunk through the other."

"So come by sometime." Kathy tried to sound offhand, as though she was ordering a pizza, but the sexy toss of her hair gave her away.

I reached up and touched her hand, or maybe just a couple of fingers. She hesitated a moment, then walked back across the park, across the street, and was devoured again by the revolving door.

11

THE ONE-O'CLOCK Diner was five blocks from the park and looked like every other diner I'd ever seen. It was close enough to the city center to be convenient and far away enough to make it less likely that you would meet the guy who worked in the next cubicle. I left my Beamer next to a large moving truck and went inside. Kathy was right about Carmen. She couldn't help being noticed. She was sitting alone in a booth and every guy in the place kept glancing her way. The four beefy moving men sitting near the door were twisting their necks to get a better view. She was intimidating—none of these guys would have the nerve to approach her. As a pole dancer she was used to stares. Her blond hair added inches to her height, and the long legs that stretched out from a short skirt added more. She appeared even taller than her six feet, and with a muscular frame she looked like she could flatten any of them with the back of her hand—and she looked as if she would enjoy it. The beefy movers who had snickered out the window at my rust spots quit grinning when I walked by them and sat down opposite the blond bombshell.

"I'm John Heron. You must be Carmen."

"You're the friend of LeRoy's, a private eye, right?" Her voice was low and husky. She kept it even lower. She didn't mind being seen but didn't want to be heard.

"Chief McGregor said I could find you here."

She looked me over, searching for some sign that would let her confide in me. "The Chief's real nice, for a cop that is. But you can't talk to the police about the police, no matter how nice they are. I think the Chief figured out that was the problem. She said I should come by here and she'd send someone over who I could trust. I guess that's you."

The waitress started toward us and Carmen quit talking. I ordered a coffee and a bowl of chicken noodle soup. After the waitress left I answered quietly, "I often deal in stuff that shouldn't see the light of day."

"Mr. Heron, I . . ."

"Blue is good."

"Blue?" She tried the word rather skeptically, then nodded and went on. "I guess I was the last person to be seen talking with Billy the night he was killed, and the police think I might know something."

"You'd been seeing him for some time. That would also get them interested."

"We had an on-and-off affair. On-and-off for quite a while. I think it was a way for both of us to get through the day. Bill didn't have many friends, if any at all, no one to talk to. Talking was more important to him than the sex. His mother died, and then he never got over that whole disaster with his father. Who would? He didn't have much of a life. I really felt kind of sorry for him." She fell quiet again as my soup and coffee arrived and we waited for the waitress to leave. "He never could run the business on his own. His father had it booming, but after Bill took over it went downhill."

"I gather his brother Jason wasn't any help."

"Jason just disappeared. He was slow anyway, and I think he started to drink, and then he got religion; then, who knows? Disappeared off the face of the earth."

I knew the financial state of Apollo Lighting. "Bill needed money to pay off debts, didn't he?"

"Yes, and he had ways of getting it." Carmen went silent again as the waitress made the rounds. She pushed her cup forward to be refilled. We sat quietly, feeling like we were being watched by everyone in the place, which was true as far as she was concerned. Carmen sipped her coffee and I stirred my soup. "I can't talk here," she said abruptly.

I agreed. "Come on. I'll drive you back to the club. We can talk in the car." I dropped some bills on the table, and included a good tip so our waitress wouldn't worry that there was something wrong with the soup. Carmen stood up, pulled herself up to her full six-feet-plus, and strode by the table of muscled gawkers. Outside, I opened the car door for her. She dropped into the bucket seat and swung her long legs in one at a time. I think she was enjoying teasing the movers who were staring out the window, or maybe it was hard for her to remember she wasn't on stage. I'm sure she made their day, although she also left enough of an impression on me to cause me to back into a hedge while turning around in the lot. We didn't say anything for the five blocks back to the center of town. I turned down the alley alongside LeRoy's, parked in the back of the lot, turned off the engine.

"Bill was blackmailing Peck!" Carmen blurted out. "I think Peck sent his goons to kill him!" Carmen sighed, as if she had just gotten a great weight off her mind. She looked down, and then, "What will you do with that?"

I avoided answering the question directly. "How much do you know? How was he blackmailing Peck?"

"I don't know. I just know that quite a bit of money kept coming down in chunks. He'd take me out to celebrate, and brag about it. I figured out that it was Peck when that Officer Weaver started hanging around. I think he was threatening Bill to get him to stop, but it didn't seem to do any good."

"But you don't know how? Blackmail is a tough charge to make with no evidence."

"I'm not trying to bring up the blackmail. What good would that do now anyway? Bill's dead. I'd just like to see that the guy who killed Bill gets what he deserves. But Blue, you've got to keep it quiet. If they thought I knew too much they'd come after me in a minute. That's why I can't tell the police, I'm sure it would get back to Peck. You understand?" She pleaded with me.

"I'll do my best," was all I could say to assure her.

"I have to go. Come see me dance, I'm on at ten tonight." Carmen swung herself out of the car and strode across the lot. She had to duck her head to get through the door to the club. Before she disappeared inside, she looked back for an instant. The fear in her eyes was in stark contrast with the sexual power of the strong tall blonde.

12

ACTION DIDN'T START AT LeRoy's for a couple of hours. I pushed the seat back, stretched out as far as the floorboard would allow, and closed my eyes. I was pretty sure that Hank had been framed and sent away for a murder he didn't commit. Bill learned that his father had contacted Hank. Bill sees his inheritance getting spread around, and he pictures Hank getting part of Apollo. He knows Hank is in town and he gets Jason to phone Hank and tell him to come see his father late at night. Bill stabs his father, leaves, waits for Hank to arrive, and points the finger. I can't prove any of that, but maybe it doesn't matter any more. Hank has served his time, guilty or not. Bill was dead and Hank had a damn good motive to kill him. Now I learn that Peck has a good reason to bump him off also, although he wouldn't do it himself. He'd send one of his bullies. Bill seems to have made a lot of enemies. I was tired of him too; I'd rather think about Carmen, and Sylvia, and Annabel, and Kathy . . . . It was dark when I woke up.

The back door of the Club wouldn't open. Carmen must have locked it behind her. I walked up the alley and around to the front. As I turned the corner I saw Stella get out of a green VW bug. I knew that car. She took only one step before she turned and leaned back down into the VW and gave the driver a kiss—a long kiss—and then hurried into the bar. I stepped back around the corner, trying to find a shadow close to the wall. This had to be the brightest intersection in town—I think it was planned that way to keep LeRoy from hiding anything. The driver waited for a moment, then put the car in gear and pulled back onto Main Street. I watched as it passed only ten feet from me and I could see the driver clearly. Sylvia was behind the wheel.

LeRoy's was crowded. A good crowd for a night at the beginning of the week. The stool at the far end of the bar was empty—my favorite spot, the gunfighter's corner, where I could watch everything and no one could sneak up behind.

LeRoy spotted me and came over with a martini in hand. "First one's on the house tonight."

"Are all bartenders good mind readers?" I asked.

"Yep. You came by to talk with Stella Starlight, right? She just went downstairs. I'll send someone down to bring her up."

I was watching LeRoy move up and down the bar, mixing drinks for the steady customers before they ordered them, giving the old-timers the knuckles on the wood that told them the drink was on the house. He was quick, efficient, and friendly, but his beard gave him away. He used to look like a mafia hit man, but now he seemed like an aging hippie. The next time he came by me I asked him, "LeRoy, were you at Woodstock?"

He stopped with a draught beer in each hand. "Me? C'mon, I was too young." Then he looked at me and smiled. "Yeah, I was there. Changed my life."

"You dance naked in the mud?"

"No, not quite. But remember Crosby, Stills and Nash—man, that was amazing! And The Grateful Dead. The Who—they started at four in the morning! I didn't go back to school after that. Thought I'd change the world. Got involved with Viet Nam protests—marches and stuff. Cops clubbed me a couple of times, hauled me in once. I wanted to change the world? Ha!" LeRoy took the beers down the bar and set them in front of two guys who should have been at home with the wife and kids. On the way back he stopped in front of me. "Fell into this bar thing after that. Just chance. Maybe now it's a smaller world that I'm changing. Look at this group. They all need help. I try. Help them escape stuff, get away. If you can't change the world, at least you might be able to escape it."

I shrugged. "I don't think I can escape. I've tried."

"No, Blue, you're different. You're an outsider, watching the world go by. You're moving parallel to time. But you can't stay out there forever. Gotta dip your toe in. You can only watch for so long, then you either come in or die of the cold. Best come in. It's not too bad." LeRoy carried two more beers down the bar.

A flaming burst of red hair announced Stella's arrival from downstairs. She started toward me, but got waylaid by three eager fans. On LeRoy's next trip to my end of the bar I asked him. "What can you tell me about Stella?"

"Well, she's only worked for us for about two months, but she's made a place for herself. You should check out the 'Music of the Spheres' sometime. She's more than amazing. I've never seen audiences so totally mesmerized. Look at those guys she's with now. They're still in a trance."

"'Music of the Spheres'? Nice title. I assume Stella studied ancient astronomy."

LeRoy answered quickly. "She *is* called Stella Starlight."

"But why 'Music of the Spheres'?" I pressed. "It's an ancient concept."

"Not sure." LeRoy thought a bit. "The music's certainly not ethereal. What's it supposed to sound like, the Music?"

"You can't hear it. It's not audible; it's just there. It's based on the rhythms of the universe. Pythagoras came up with it."

"Isn't he that right-triangle guy who helped me flunk geometry?"

"Yep. Same guy. He looked at the cycles of the planets. Compared them to one another and came up with frequencies, vibrations that could not be heard, but they established a harmony throughout the universe. Some people say that Adam and Eve destroyed that harmony when they went for the apple; some people say it's still there; some people say it's B flat; some people say it's a lot of bunk."

LeRoy was interested. "All I can say is that the music of her spheres sure knocks 'em dead. And she's got rhythm. I wouldn't want to lose her."

"So what's the connection with Hank? Business?"

Someone caught LeRoy's eye and he turned to mix up three concoctions that required cherries and tiny umbrellas. He kept talking over his shoulder. "I don't think that's business. There's something between them, although it seems a bit explosive."

LeRoy took off to deliver the drinks. I nursed the martini and thought of Sylvia. Yes, cute. No wonder she wasn't moved by my irresistible charm—she was hooked on Stella. I looked up to check on Stella Starlight. I caught her eye and she nodded, left her fans and came over to my end of the bar.

"Please join me." I motioned to a stool as if it were a fine dining room chair. She slid on to it as though she was sliding around a silver pole. Her knees brushed slowly along my thigh as she swiveled toward the bar. LeRoy brought a seltzer over without being asked. The professionals dance better when sober—the rest of us dance better when stewed to the gills.

"Stella. How are you? Don't see you much at The Arms."

Stella answered warmly. "Guess we keep different hours, but I hear you coming and going. You should stop in sometime." Then Stella's smile became more professional. "What can I help you with?" There was always the chance that a light conversation might lead to something more.

"I'm trying to locate Hank Menotti. You know him."

"Not well. Met him a couple of times," she said without interest.

"You were talking with him Sunday night, I understand. Here in the bar."

Stella wasn't forthcoming. She lived in a parallel universe that started with the body, then moved inevitably toward sex. The mundane details that made up most of our lives were irrelevant. "I talk to a lot of men." She tossed her head to fling a rebellious strand of red hair into the air. I watched it float slowly back into place.

"I gather you got into a bit of an argument."

Stella shot an accusing glance at LeRoy. "Seems a gal can't turn an offer down without it becoming public knowledge."

LeRoy apologized with a shrug of his shoulders.

"Just business?" I asked.

"Yes, just business. We have to keep our standards." A sharp edge crept into her voice. Her knee moved away from my leg.

That line of questioning wasn't going any further. I took another tack. "You've got beautiful hair."

Stella looked surprised. "Well, thank you." She smiled suspiciously, waiting for me to explain.

"Used to be black, didn't it?"

"That's not a nice thing to say to a girl." Stella pushed the half-finished seltzer away and reached for her purse. "Just what are you getting at anyway?"

"No offense. It looked good."

"How would you know?" She slid away from me and off the stool.

"It was black when you came to the Windsore funeral."

Stella's lips tightened. "I wasn't at any funeral. You know I moved up here about two months ago."

I took the color photograph Ms. Lente had copied for me from my inside pocket, unfolded it, and laid it on the bar. "You're too pretty to stay inconspicuous, even in the background. Nice hair, very black. But you don't look too happy to be there."

Stella said nothing.

"We should talk?" I suggested.

"Not now. Not here. Come by my apartment sometime and we can talk, if you still want to." Stella turned to leave. "Don't expect me to tell you anything, but we can chat or whatever. Carmen is about to dance, and I'm next. Have to go put on my costume."

I had no doubt that her costume involved more taking off than putting on. Stella's fans parted like the waters of the Red Sea as she moved toward the entrance to the downstairs Club. She turned and looked at me for a second before disappearing through the door, sucking energy from the room as she left. LeRoy stopped in the midst of shaking a martini, shook his head and said, "She's a mystery. A beautiful mystery."

I complimented LeRoy. "Between Stella and Carmen, you've got some striking women on your hands. How do you do it?"

LeRoy smiled. "I don't do anything. They come to me. Maybe it's the fine benefits that come with the job."

"And maybe it's because you leave them alone. Ever check on their past lives?"

LeRoy laughed. "You think I ask for letters of recommendation before I hire a stripper? I do have to keep something on record—a name, an address, social security number. I wouldn't vouch for the accuracy, 'cept maybe for the first name. And that doesn't last very long. Do you think mom comes up with Stella Starlight or Dee Dee Darling for her little girl?"

"Anything else?"

"Okay. I see what you're getting at. Maybe I have something but I doubt it, and if I did, my girls can't know that I give this stuff to anybody. They all have pasts. If the police come by, I'll have to give them what I have, but it ain't much. Promise me you won't send them over."

"Scout's honor." I raised my left hand, then my right.

LeRoy shook his head. "Boy scout, my ass!"

I gulped down the remains of the martini. "I think I'll go down and watch Carmen. Judging by the string of horny guys that have been going that way, she must have a skeleton key to their groins."

"More like a key to their wallets." LeRoy took out a scrap of paper from under the bar and wrote something on it. "Here, give this to the ticket guy. Get you in free. Just don't let on that you've got anything to do with the police force."

I joined the line to the Club. After the first door I handed the paper to the ticket guy and opened the second. The noise that burst through explained why two doors were necessary. Music, laughter, hollering, and the show hadn't even started.

The club was darker than I remembered from yesterday afternoon, perhaps because the stage was bright. It was lit by spotlights hidden behind a circle of red curtain that dropped a couple of feet from the ceiling. On the outside of the circle a series of bulbs pulsated with color. Another ring of lights circled the foot of the stage. The dancing surface was higher than the tables to assure that the dancers towered over the patrons, but low enough to allow the guys to stuff tips into g-strings. Tonight the four poles glowed like silver columns rising to the heavens. As my eyes grew used to the dark surrounding the stage, I could see the crowd. Not bad for a weekday night. On all sides of the stage were small tables, each with a flickering electric candle. Just enough light for the patrons to count out the money to pay for their drinks. Around the outer wall of the room were couches fitted into booths for the patrons who would sacrifice proximity to the dancing flesh for a bit of anonymity. I moved along the back of the room. I didn't want to be recognized, but a six-foot-two private eye doesn't blend in easily. I slid to the back of a small booth next to the door, caught the eye of a partially dressed roaming waitress, and ordered a beer. Martinis were not served in strip clubs. They didn't want anyone to draw comparisons between their dancers and Fred Astaire.

A master of ceremonies, who doubled as the bouncer, appeared on stage. The guy was tall and ripped and must be the guy Kathy spent some time with. Damn! He silenced the crowd and announced the first act of the evening. "Tonight we are proud to present the fabulous Carmen! Let's give her a big hand!" This was greeted with a smattering of applause and a couple of hoots. The crowd was still relatively sober. Carmen strutted out and took ownership of the audience before the music started. On the elevated stage and sporting a pair of six-inch-high heels she looked down at the rowdy crowd like a teacher looks at a class of noisy kindergarten kids. She glowed with a gold waist-length jacket, gold bikini, blond hair, bronze skin, and enough tassels to line the pope's robe. Motley Crue's 'Girls, Girls, Girls' blasted from the speakers. The music was painfully loud—conversation was not the main event—and Carmen began to gyrate. She aimed her shaking breasts, swiveling hips, and smiles at chosen targets at the tables. The jacket came off quickly and she started sliding up and down a pole as if she was making love to Mr. Stick Figure. She was a powerful woman, strong enough to hold on to the pole and swing her body around and away from it. The smile never wavered. She had summed up the crowd with a professional eye and selected two gentlemen in the front row as prime targets.

The waitress returned with my beer. I gave her a twenty and told her to keep the change. I thought she was going to climb into my lap right then—it was easy to buy good graces in a strip club. Twenty bucks to buy a lap dance, the perfection of frustration. Now that I could see better, I spotted a couple of the girls working the back booths—a lap dance and maybe a date for later. Carmen's bra had found a new owner by now, who thought that putting it on his head was the funniest thing ever. Her nipples were covered only by pasties with swinging tassels. In classic stripper pose, she stood with hands on her hips and started the tassels spinning, first together, and then in opposite directions. Always an impressive skill. The motion of the tassels put one of the front row admirers into an hypnotic trance and he kept reaching forward to stuff dollar bills in the waist band of the all-but-nonexistent bikini. He was so far gone, I could have sat on his lap and gotten back my twenty.

Figures moving in the dark, macho overtures, guilty advances. Men trying to be seen; men hoping they weren't seen. Some flirting with the muscular bouncer. Waitresses moved about, plying alcohol. Lap dancers worked the dark alcoves. Carmen had won over the crowd with a pole dance that kept all eyes focused on her g-string.

A couple of guys hiding in a back booth looked familiar. I recognized them from the Police Department motor pool and I thought I'd better leave before I spoiled their party. Carmen was finishing up her act. The last remnant of modesty had come off and she was spinning it over her head and was about to fling it into the audience when I slipped out the back door.

LeRoy had a pretty strict code concerning the action on the premises—no prostitution on site. The parking lot outside, however, was an uncontrolled free-for-all. LeRoy didn't own it. It belonged to the city. The cars were containers for sex, or whatever we humans substituted for sex. Those who had the means would drive off for extended trysts in a nearby motel. I walked by a pick-up truck with fogged windows, and the action inside a tan Chevy wagon was testing its shock absorbers. I drove up the alley, turned onto Main, and headed home with an empty seat beside me.

13

Hank menotti was out of prison and back in town, and causing trouble, if not murder. I wanted to find him. The best place to start would be where I last saw him. I'd left the Club and was driving north on Main. Route 22 was ahead, the highway that led north through the State Forest. On a hunch I turned. The road wandered through the upscale section of town, distinguished by recently built McMansions. All signs of human frailty had been banned: no cars in the driveway, no laundry on a line, no dogs, no litter, no bikes, no life. At the edge of town the streetlights ended, and I began to watch closely for the turn onto Merrimac Road. I hadn't been back to the Windsore estate since the day he was murdered, and things had changed a lot. The pavement of the winding driveway had broken into chunks, and no longer did sensors trigger a series of lights to lead me in. Winter's cold and summer's heat had been wreaking havoc on the tar for years; now it lay in bits that sprang up behind the front wheels and banged into the underside of the Beamer. The estate remained deserted. Nobody would buy it and nobody took care of it. It had entered into teenage lore as a haunted house where a mad couple could be seen wandering naked through the rooms at night. The original Victorian was comfortable with the neglect, as it was from an earlier age and was accustomed to being ignored. The once-modern additions hadn't done as well. The windows of the modern wing were cracked or broken entirely. The doors had fallen off the garage; all that remained inside were rusted car parts and a couple of broken lawnmowers. The cracked wood and peeling paint on the two Palladium columns bracketing the front porch made the roof look dangerously unstable. There was no moon, and the Victorian's sharply sloped roof rose as a tall shadow, barely visible against a gloomy sky. A screech owl howled and sent shivers into the night. The sound of metal sliding on metal. Rust against rust. The sound of metal against bone. A blue Toyota, a rental, sat by the porch. One lonely light shone through shutters closed over an upstairs window. I gave JJ a quick call on my cell before approaching the house.

I waded through tall weeds that had replaced the lawn and stepped over a dead tree which lay across the front steps. In the dark it was difficult to get to the front door as most of the porch had rotted away. I moved quietly around to the side. The boards that had covered the side door had been ripped away. A night creature scurried over the edge of crushed metal flashing, and a thump came from inside. With a push, the broken door creaked open, and I felt my way across the living room to the stairs. I followed the path that JJ and I had taken twelve years ago. Through a dark living room, up the stairs and along the hall to the room where the light was coming from. I thought that the creaking boards would alert him, but when I looked into the bedroom, a thin figure in jeans and a brown leather jacket sat motionless on the floor at the foot of the big four-poster. The only furnishings left in the room were the bed and mattress, a chair turned on its side, and a large empty armoire with its doors hanging open. The mattress was stained and moldy. Small creatures had moved in, had chewed holes through the fabric, and had carried off chunks of its insides. An electric lantern rested on the floor. Its light threw a large shadow of a huddled figure onto the far wall. I'd guessed right. Hank Menotti had returned to the scene of the crime.

"Mr. Menotti?" I said quietly.

Hank jumped. "Who the fuck are you?"

"John Heron. I met you here twelve years ago. What are you doing back again?"

"This place is rent free, maybe I'll move in," Hank growled. "There's plenty of space and some company, if you don't mind ghosts. I never knew them when they were alive—maybe now's my chance to get acquainted." Hank studied me for a moment, leaned forward and said with accusation in his voice, "I remember you now. You're that private eye guy. You won't understand—you're part of the crowd that put me away." His motion caused the head of the shadow to grow larger on the wall behind him.

"And you came back to visit your father, and maybe also Billy?"

"Fuck! If I saw that trash again I'd slit his throat."

I waited. I could see he wanted to get his story out, even to me.

"Look, flatfoot! I just spent twelve years in the pen for something I didn't do. I got plenty of reason to be pissed!"

"You think Bill framed you?"

"I don't think, I know! But you guys couldn't give a shit about that! He and Jason set it up, and set me up. And if I ever meet either of them, I'll . . . I'll . . . ."

"How about stabbing him in the back? That works pretty well."

Hank looked at me and snarled. "What are you getting at, private dick-face? You have something to tell me?"

"Your half-brother is dead. Two nights ago. But you know that, don't you?"

He ignored my accusation. "What do you mean dead? What happened?"

"You trying to tell me you don't know. It's not exactly a secret. Everybody in the town knows."

"Well, dammit, I wasn't in town. I went to see my mom yesterday."

"Where's your mom?"

"Fuck you!" Hank stared at the floor. "What do I care anyway? Serves him right, but what . . . what are you getting at?" Hank stumbled on the words, his tough façade was beginning to crumble. "You think I did it, don't you?"

"It doesn't look like you have much of an alibi, and you've been piling up motives ever since you drove back into this town."

Hank pointed a finger at me and shouted, "I had nothing to do with this, you son-of-a-bitch! And there's no way I'm going back behind bars. They framed me once. It isn't going to happen again. Now get the fuck out of here, or are you thinking of winning a medal and taking me down to the station?" Hank slumped back against the foot of the bed; his shadow morphed into a large formless lump.

I turned the one chair in the room upright, and sat down. Hank huddled on the floor and scowled and wasn't planning to say any more. Like an invisible fog, a stillness inhabited the room. The house fell into a deathly quiet, and the air was becoming too thin to breathe. That was when the ghosts arrived. A rustle of sheets, a cold draft, the shutters swung open and then banged shut. George and Mary Windsore, Mother and Dad, sat up in the big four-poster. They were both naked—naked ghosts. They didn't look too scary, as he hadn't been stabbed yet. No scars, no blood. I doubt that ghosts bleed. She cast the sheet aside, and they sat side by side in the bed looking at me. She smiled and spread her legs slightly. He patted the bed between them, inviting me to join. I could see clear through their shapes to the rumpled sheets and pillows. He gestured again, with a translucent hand. Bare from head to toe, his vaporous cock appeared to be both hard and soft at the same time. They were both smiling at me now. A threesome, with ghosts. Should I undress? Must I also be a ghost? Will I become a ghost? What will I feel when I touch them? I wanted to find out, and she was sexy, and . . . .

"Why don't you get the fuck out of here and leave me alone?" Hank interrupted.

I hesitated before answering, but then went back to the subject. "You never met your father?" I gestured at the empty mattress.

"No. Never met him, never saw him when he was alive." Hank shuddered. "It was horrible. Blood everywhere."

"Hank, I dug up a lot of stuff at the library. This may come as a surprise, but I agree with you. The trial did seem to be a sham, at least to the extent there was a trial." Hank listened, and I went on. "Peck needed you. He needed a victory to back up his image as a tough prosecutor. He didn't care whether you were guilty or not—you were a means to an end." Hank visibly thawed as I went over the details. He leaned back and his face melted into tears. I waited a bit and then, "Why did you come here that night, if you didn't intend to kill him?"

He sighed, resigned. "I told the cops. They wouldn't believe me. You know he was my father—deserted my mother before I ever got to know him, or even meet him. I think he began to feel guilty. He'd lost his wife that year and maybe that reminded him that he was mortal. My mother was struggling so hard to make it work, going from job to job. She finally joined the church, started doing charity work. It kept her going. Then he called. He called me, can you imagine that? First time I'd heard anything from my father. I didn't even know he was alive. He wanted to make amends for the whole thing the only way he knew, with his money. We were broke, so I came up and checked in at the motel. I got a call that evening. He said I should come by around 10:30 that night."

"But he went to bed early. Would he be half naked in bed if he was expecting you?" I looked back at the bed. The ghosts had vanished.

"That's what the DA asked. But it wasn't my father who called. It was Jason, my half-brother, who said my father wanted to see me that night. When I got here, he was dead. You saw that. I was set up. The bastards!" The story had haunted Hank for years. He was relieved to tell it to someone who might actually believe him.

"You pleaded guilty to manslaughter. If you were innocent, why?"

"Are you kidding? With that DA out to get me? You said it: I was the reason he got elected. If I ever get my hands on him I'll . . ." Hank grabbed at a throat his mind had formed in the air—the large hands of his shadow grabbed at the wall. "He charged me with the first degree. That's life at best and I didn't have any alibi, or witnesses, nothing. Not to mention that his bodyguards were very good at persuasion. I took the plea. Twelve years with good behavior. Tell me, did I have a choice?"

"Maybe not," I agreed, but kept up the pressure. "Why did you come back now?"

"I don't know. To see the place I guess, or maybe we came just to say goodbye."

"We?"

"What we?" Hank barked. "Me. I came by. What's wrong with that? You're beginning to piss me off. Look, asshole, I learned some tough stuff in the pen. Don't tempt me to use it on you." Hank struggled to his feet.

I was tempted to see what techniques were taught in prison, but I could see Hank was about to fall apart. Tears were streaming down his cheeks and his hands were trembling and he was having trouble just standing up. I stepped aside and encouraged him to move toward the door. "We have to go to the precinct. It'll just be for questioning. Don't worry, they've got nothing on you for Bill's murder, but you do have to answer some questions. You need to explain why you're here."

Hank picked up the lantern and we found our way back down the stairs. As we crossed the living room, a light from the outside swept by the shuttered windows, sending bright streaks over us and the far wall.

"You've brought someone!" Hank's accusing whisper cut the dark.

We watched through the slats as a squad car pulled up behind my car. The driver's door opened and an overweight cop swiveled his stomach from under the steering wheel. I recognized Peck's driver, Kozimov, the overstuffed dumpling. The passenger door opened and The Weevil stepped out. Hank turned as white as a Klu Klux Clan meeting. His fear filled the room and made me shiver. The Weevil and Officer Dumpling stepped to opposite sides of the patrol car, both with revolvers drawn. "Come on out! Hands over your head! It's the police! Don't try anything stupid!"

"No way," Hank whispered. He was shivering. "They worked me over once—it ain't gonna happen again."

"I'll take care of it," I assured him. "Let's go. Follow me."

"No," Hank pleaded.

I stepped out the side door pulling Hank behind me. "Hold it guys. He's unarmed, and I'm working with you. I've got it under control. You can put down the weapons." I stepped into the glare of the headlights; Hank stayed behind me.

"Put your hands high, Menotti!" growled Weevil. "Heron, get the fuck out of the way."

"Take it easy, officer." I tried to calm the situation. "There's no danger here." I pushed a terrified Hank toward my car.

Weevil stopped us. "Move out of the way, Heron!" He reached around and grabbed Hank by the arm, twisted it, and threw him to the ground. Hank started to get up but Driver Dumpling gave him a hard kick in the side, and he crumpled over.

"Too much, guys!" I shouted. "Put the guns down. I'm taking him in. This is . . ."

Dumpling pulled out a pair of cuffs and grabbed one of Hank's wrists. Hank struggled, terrified, and began flailing his arms. Weevil swung his pistol and caught Hank in the shoulder. He started to swing again, aiming for the head, when I stepped behind the cop, put one arm around his waist and pulled him back against me. With my other hand I grabbed the barrel of the pistol and pushed it down. Dumpling swung toward me with his pistol pointed right at me. Actually it was pointed right at Weevil as I held him in front of me. Hank didn't hesitate. He jumped up and ran, using the patrol car for a shield. Dumpling turned and raised his pistol, aiming at the retreating Hank. I shoved Weevil into him and the shot exploded into the front tire of the patrol car. The tire hissed and belched and the car sank into an awkward tilt. "Fucking idiot!" Dumpling swore. Weevil backed off and raised his pistol with two hands, setting up for a shot at the fleeing Hank when he was blinded by the headlights that turned the corner. A loudspeaker crackled over the scene. "Superintendent Cakes here. Put away the guns. Nobody's going to get hurt here."

Weevil ignored the call and raced around his patrol car after Hank, who was deep into the forest by now. Dumpling started after him, but ran out of breath after thirty feet. Officer Corbutt appeared with JJ, a calm island in the midst of chaos. A series of sharp snaps crackled through the night air. Hank was gone and Weevil was standing at the edge of the clearing firing randomly into the woods. Something had moved and he emptied his pistol in the direction of some big-eyed night creature and missed him, too. I leaned against the front of Hank's blue rental and looked down. There was a scrape across the front bumper. The screech owl wailed again, Hank had escaped, JJ pushed his hands into his pockets and frowned, and I was in deep shit.

14

I WASTED THURSDAY TURNING THE case over in my mind until the facts began to run together like the ice and gin in an abandoned martini on the rocks. Yesterday, I had decided that Hank didn't kill Bill. Then after I let him escape, I spot the scratch on the bumper of the car he rented. It was a blue car just like the one I nicked in the Three Bears' parking lot. Puts him right back at the scene of the crime. If he goes back to the motel in Tungsten, JJ's guy will pick him up. I doubt he'll show up there. I should find him before he does something stupid. And where the hell is Bill's brother Jason now? Then we've got Hank and Stella fighting about something, and Bill hanging out with Carmen, and Peck with a motive, and Weevil and Dumpling showing up at all the wrong times.

The call from the precinct came at the end of the day, and it didn't come from a friend. It was Flint, Kathy's front man. He came right to the point with apparent relish. I was ordered to lay low and stay away from anybody and anything to do with the murder. Flint's self-importance was easy to read, but between the lines I could also spot Kathy's disappointment. She stood up for me in front of the DA, but my resume of fuck-ups seemed to just keep growing. She was the new head police honcho, Chief McGregor, and it was a tough way for her to start off.

Night had crept up on me, a quiet night. A heavy fog had rolled in and hidden the train yards, the tracks that provide the material for my wandering dreams. The air is stifling; the low clouds are keeping the asphalt plant fumes close to the ground and close to my window. I should call Kathy, but I think she's given up on me. I don't blame her for that. Maybe I'll send some flowers tomorrow. That would blow her mind. I'd have to sneak them past the precinct security desk. She'd have to hide them under her desk. I might not be too romantic but I sure beat the police department. Damn! There goes Eddie's music. Might be tolerable if I could hear the whole song, but this old wall only allows the beat to come through. *Thump* . . . *Thump* . . . *Thump*. I'll give him a half hour and then climb through the window and turn it off. Wonder what Sylvia is up to tonight. I'm not depraved enough to sneak along the fire escape and spy in her window—I'll have to do all the spying in my mind. She dresses to keep her body well hidden, but maybe librarians have to or else all the teenage boys in the world would never learn anything from a book. 3B's door slammed a while ago. Stella's home—must be her night off. No stripping tonight, so she can pick up a little extra-curricular money at home. Yes, she's brought one home tonight, that was fast, the pounding has begun. *Thud*

... *Thud* ... *Thud*. Couldn't she move the head of the bed away from the wall? Every time the john pounds forward my collection of martini glasses shimmies dangerously toward the edge of the bar. *Thump* ... *Thump* from Eddie's stereo. *Thud* ... *Thud* from Stella's humper. Now the beats are getting in sync. Maybe I can rub a bit in sync, make it a trio, take my mind off the world. I close my eyes and let my mind and my hand wander. *Thump* ... *Thud* ... *Mmm* ... *Thump* ... *Thud* ... *Mmm*.

I am in the library. Kathy's there too. We're leafing through a pile of art books, and she is pointing out the beauties of the nude goddesses. Then she begins to take the positions. A lovely scene on the edge of the forest. We're sitting on a blanket, a picnic in the afternoon. Kathy has undressed, her clothes piled behind her. She hands me a sandwich. *Thump* ... *Thud* ... *Mmm* ... *Thump* ... *Thud* .. . *Mmm* ... *Thump* ... *CRACK* ... *Thud* ... *Thump* ... *Thud*.

What the fuck was that? I've heard gunshots before; they have a sound that one doesn't forget easily. Where? The thumping continues. The thudding continues. I imagine the smell of blood mixing with the asphalt fumes. Sounded like the shot came from the direction of Eddie's room. I'm out the window, along the fire escape, and looking into his apartment. He's slumped, as usual, but not in the chair. He's on the floor twisted like a discarded oil rag. There's no one else in the room. I climb in through the window, careful not to step in the bits of blood and pieces of brain scattered around the floor. Eddie's body appears to grow smaller as the pool of blood grows larger. The booming radio can't cover the strange quiet of the room. I try to find a pulse, not that I expect any sign of life on someone with a small hole in the front of his head, and a large one in the back.

I move to the door to his bedroom, kick it open and jump aside. No one's there; no one's in the bathroom; no one's in the apartment. I turn off the radio and study the room. The crucifix on the wall is surrounded by spattered blood. It remains untouched. Booze and religion—Eddie seemed to have found a way to follow both paths. The front door to his apartment is closed—I open it to see an empty hallway. I run down the hall and the two flights to the lobby. When I reach the bottom of the stairs, no one's in the lobby. Javier's door is open so he could keep watch, but he was preoccupied watching a soccer match on the tube. He looks up, looks out the door of his living room, looks with a concerned eye at a shouting guy wearing only a pair of jockey shorts.

"Did you see anybody? Did anyone leave?" I yell.

"Guys have been coming and going all evening, Mr. Heron." Javier doesn't lose his calm composure.

"Just now, did you?"

"Some guy, yes."

"Who?"

"Don't know. Some guy in a raincoat and a hat, I think. What's the trouble?"

"Eddie's been shot! He's dead!"

"*Puta madre!*"

I'm at the front steps of The Arms in time to see taillights disappear around the corner by the cemetery. No way to catch up with that—and I don't have my car keys anyway, and I'd just locked myself out my place, and Eddie's dead, and I am in my underwear.

"Jesus, Blue! Next door! What the hell were you thinking!" JJ was sputtering and turning a dangerous shade of red. "You should have known they were coming for him."

Javier had let me back into my place so I could get a pair of pants and a shirt. He had opened Eddie's door for the cops, and JJ and I were standing over Eddie's lifeless body.

"Coming for Eddie? What are you talking about?"

"I'm talking about this corpse. I'm talking about Jason Windsore. I'm talking about the brother of the guy who was murdered last week. I'm talking about the guy who was shot about six feet away from you while you're, while you're what, I don't know?" JJ was clearly flustered.

"His name is Eddie," I protested. "Eddie Jones."

"Jason Windsore, you idiot! You're telling me you didn't know who he was?"

"Not a clue." *Not a clue?* I thought: drunk, dropped out, a crucifix on the wall, and I don't figure out who he is. No wonder I'm not getting jobs as a private eye.

"You remember the trial. Remember the murders?"

"I wasn't at the trial, JJ. I never saw this guy before. He moved in here a couple of years ago, and as far as I know never did anything but sit here and drink."

Kathy and Officer Corbutt walked in. I knew she was upset when she got formal with me. "Mr. Heron, why don't you just go back to 3C and try to stay there. JJ, you take this floor and see who's here and what they know. Corbutt, you stay here. I'll take the second floor. Nobody touch anything in this room. She turned and walked out. JJ looked at me and then walked down the hall. Corbutt shoved his hands into his pockets and shrugged. I quit feeling sorry for Eddie and began feeling sorry for myself. Eddie was dead and it looks like that's what he wanted. I'd lost the trust of my friends and that's not what I wanted.

15

I SLEPT IN AS LONG as I could to avoid a visit to Police headquarters. It was noon before I braced myself with three cups of coffee and faced the inevitable. I drove to the precinct to give my side of the story. Officer Corbutt was assigned to question me and dutifully wrote down everything I remembered. I'd missed some clue that would have told me that Eddie Jones was Jason Windsore, but I wasn't the only one. He'd quit working at Apollo Lighting years ago, and dropped out of sight. I'd never seen the guy when he was still called Jason. As far as I could tell from the photographs, he never even turned up for his parents' funeral. Billy probably sent him money for rent and booze. It wasn't hard to imagine the demons that haunted Jason; he apparently had a role in the murder of his father. I didn't doubt that older brother Bill was behind the whole thing. He hated his father. His father beat him up when he was a kid. Then he was about to lose a chunk of his inheritance to the bastard child that came from his father's playing around. He got Jason, who wasn't too bright, to make the call to Hank. That made Jason an accessory to the crime, which assured that he'd keep quiet. Bill murders his father, leaves, then returns to pin it on Hank. He didn't expect to find JJ and me there, but that just helped his case. Hank was a sitting duck and he took the rap. Now, twelve years later, Hank gets out of prison and Bill and Jason are both murdered. I'd better find Hank, and I'd better find him soon.

I finished with Corbutt and left the station. Kathy and JJ were nowhere to be seen. I walked back across the street to the park, found my bench where I could watch the pigeons. Where to look for Hank? How about his mother? Worth a try. Tomorrow I'll take a drive out to Libertyville and try the churches. Maybe someone will know Mrs. Menotti, maybe she'll still be there somewhere, maybe she can tell me she's seen Hank, maybe I could win the lottery. I looked forward to getting out of town for a day. A ray of sun found a gap in the clouds and warmed the air, but it still left my insides cold. I could see dark clouds on the horizon, moving rapidly in from the west. The storm would hit in about an hour, and I decided to stay on the bench and wait for it.

If your goal is boredom, the best thing to do is to drive west out of our town. You'll find yourself on one long straight turnpike to eternity. The ramps don't wait for you to clear the city limits. They spiral up about fifteen blocks beyond the Main Street Mall. The on-ramp spins you around 180° and back 90° to get to a multilevel figure eight that successfully obliterates any sense of direction. Miss the overhead lane-changing instructions and you'll find yourself hurtling south with no chance to change your mind for twenty miles. Make the right choice and you can lead-foot your car up to sixty miles per hour before the ramp squeezes it into a lane filled with kamikaze trucks with eighteen wheels that substitute air horns for brakes. You're on the Interstate headed west. Pick a lane and jack the car up another twenty miles an hour to stay with the traffic and that's the last decision you have to make for hours. There's not much to look at, mostly trees and every so often the backs of houses who've been condemned to a 24-hour perpetual roar. Eventually, with the speedometer pointing to eighty, the car feels stationary. Einstein's theory is demonstrated by the road, the trees, and the houses rushing by your window in the opposite direction. The driver falls into a trance where any urge to slow down, to stop for a bite to eat or take a bathroom break is an act of treason. The bladder becomes an annoyance to be defeated. Next rest stop thirty-three miles. I'll skip this one; I can hold it in until then. I finally give in, turn into the John Quincy Adams Rest Area—rest areas are named after Presidents and football coaches—and I'm still traveling at fifty miles-per-hour when I screech into the parking area. There is a law that requires all rest stops in the country to look exactly the same and serve the same food. JQ Adams doesn't disappoint. I take a coffee and a burger back to the car and, when I'm back up to eighty, begin eating lunch. I manage not to spill the coffee but I do leave a catsup stain on my pants, which won't help my chances on this trip to find true love.

Exit 53, three and one half hours. I rolled off the thruway, down the exit ramp and on to a four-lane highway. After twenty miles I turned on to a two-lane highway, then on to a series of blacktop roads that got steadily narrower and wound through fields of corn and barley, or rye, or whatever that tall grass is. What I do know is that if you rot it long enough it turns into a drink that will do the same for your insides. A sign announced my goal—Entering Libertyville—and another announcing that Libertyville was a DRUG FREE ZONE. That's a relief. It was a small wooden-house town, which had seen better days when the farms were in full swing. I passed a trailer park on the way in and some houses where the residents were apparently rich enough to own two or three cars but not rich enough to buy a new tire or scrape the leaves off the windshield. Toward the center of Libertyville a few larger houses spoke of a bygone civic pride, but they too needed paint and a lot of new glass. Along Main Street, at least I assumed it was called Main Street, there was a row of two-story buildings with shops on the ground floor, and a few residents were there to get a haircut, a beauty treatment, or some pain killers. No doubt there was a large shopping mall outside of town that had stolen the customers. The street led to a small circle that surrounded a larger-than-life-sized statue of a general whose main function was to provide a space for the pigeons to sit and patina the bronze. On the north side of the circle was a church. I had reached my destination. Now to see if it was worth the trip.

The Church of The Holy Father of His Holiness stood by the circle with a quiet confidence, aloof from the daily humdrum of the small town. The two large doors were not open and had not been opened for years. One entered through a smaller door to the right, turned and pushed open a second door. With that entrance you crossed the Atlantic Ocean and dropped back a few hundred years in time. The inside was quiet, cool, a different universe from the outside. Rows of empty benches flanked a long aisle down the middle. It ended with a low wooden railing before the altar at the far end. A ray of sunlight beamed through from the cupola high above, the dusty air giving the beam a ghostly substance. Behind the altar hung the crucified man, Christ, suffering, suffering for my sins as if I didn't suffer enough on my own. The church was deserted. No men in long robes with tassels swinging pots of incense, coating the air with a heavy fragrance. No one chanting prayers in Latin that were best left untranslated. No organ tones rising from all parts of the church simultaneously, and no choir to send angelic voices over the worshippers with hymns that were never written but passed down through generations. No single file of the devout lined up to receive a wafer on their tongue and sip from the cup, the chalice, that many others had drunk from. On Sunday the rituals would occur in unison, the audience rising to their feet, kneeling, sitting back down, picking up the hymnbooks and opening them to the specified page. Ritual, tradition, ceremony, theatre—in Latin. Keep the ceremony, and the stranger the better. Theatre in another tongue, indecipherable and curious. Throw out the moral certainty, scrap the unforgiving definition of good and evil, banish the guilt. I like the church; I just don't like the religion. So forget about enforcing the separation of church and state—I'm for the separation of church and religion.

A figure in black materialized from behind the altar and was moving around, checking the position of the props for the next service or looking for the Bible he left somewhere during the last rites. I approached him with a "Good morning, Father."

He nodded with a gentle 'what can I do for you' expression.

"I was hoping you could help me. I'm looking for a Mrs. Menotti. I think she is a member of your congregation, or at least was a number of years ago. Perhaps she ran a women's auxiliary or a charity."

"Mrs. Menotti," he repeated. "How long ago do you think it was?"

"It would be about ten years." I could see that the name was not ringing a bell.

"No. I wouldn't know her. I've only been here a few years. But there is a priest who has been here forever. He might remember her."

"He's here somewhere?" I asked.

"Yes, in the parish house in back." He hesitated before giving me the name. "Father Flannigan."

"Mind if I go back there?"

He pointed toward a door behind the altar. "Just one thing. Father Flannigan is a bit on the far side, if you know what I mean. But he is harmless."

I thanked him and went out without the slightest idea of what he meant. A small wooden house was squeezed in behind the church. I knocked. No answer. I knocked again. I heard someone move inside so I stepped to the window beside the door and tried to peer in. It was dark and I put my face close to the glass. There was a face on the other side of the glass staring into my eyes with the look of a mad devil. I jumped back. "Jesus Christ!"

The window flew open, the head appeared, and Father Flannigan cried out, "Jesus, pray to Jesus, Jesus the Lord."

"I wasn't exactly praying . . ."

The window crashed shut, the door was thrown open, and a small hooded figure in black aimed a pair of intense gray eyes at me. He pointed a knobby finger in my face and started his sermon. "Christ is the Lord. Christ the Savior. Let us pray." He fell to his knees, motioning me to follow.

"It's not exactly my thing, Father. I mean . . ."

"Of course it is. I heard you. You called out to Jesus. Now let us go to Him." He kept waving me toward the ground. "You cried out to Jesus. Now let us find Him."

I protested. "When you lose your keys, you cry out to Jesus. You have to lose your mind to find Jesus."

Father Flannigan worked his way up to a semi-upright position. Standing, he was a foot and a half shorter than me. He face changed from fire and brimstone to disappointment. I had ruined his chance to save a soul. "If you're not here to find Jesus, you're here to find one of the chosen. Lord be praised. So tell me, my heathen friend, who might that be?"

I'd been promoted from the category of "burn in hell" to one of "heathen friend." A step in the right direction. "A good woman, a Mrs. Menotti. She was one of your flock some years ago. Did good work. I would like to find her, take her news of her son." Actually I was hoping she had news of her son to give to me, but I figured that was close enough.

"Very sad, very sad. The Lord has come for her."

I was startled, "She has died?"

"No. But the Lord has taken her mind. The body is still with us, but the mind has found a place in heaven. May it rest in peace."

"And where does the mindless body remain now, good Father?" I asked.

"Mother Superior keeps the body now. Sisters of Mercy, up on the hill. I must pray now. Come with me and pray to Jesus." He began shuffling for the back door to the church, waving his hand over his head for me to follow.

I decided to take my chances of finding Mrs. Menotti without Jesus's help and walked around front to the circle. A stop in a candy store didn't get me much information, but I did pick up a box of chocolates. The guy at the hardware store didn't speak too much English; I wondered how he ended up in Libertyville. The owner of the dress store next door was more helpful. I followed her directions through the small streets of the town until the Sisters of Mercy Home for the Aged and Infirm rose on a hill before me. From a distance it stood as grand as a Lord's estate. I drove between two stone columns flanking the entrance and followed a long curved drive that wound through a couple of acres of mowed lawn. As I neared the Home, I could see on a side terrace figures moving slowly. Some in wheelchairs, some accompanied by women in nurses' uniforms or black nuns' habits. Everyone moved in slow motion. The large parking lot on the other side was mostly empty, but there was a clearly marked hierarchy of spaces. I passed the emergency parking, the staff-only spaces, the wheelchair and handicapped parking, to settle into the row farthest from the door.

The front entrance was pretending to be a church. A circular window with a stained-glass scene of angels, some Latin script engraved around the edges, presided over large wooden doors. Inside was a disappointment. A bare room with swinging double doors on both sides to accommodate gurneys, and a large desk in the middle. Behind the desk sat a stern-faced woman in full Mother Superior garb. Behind her stood a young nun with bright eyes and dark black hair peeking out from her cap. The Mother Superior gave me an 'I can see you're not a believer' once-over and went back to filling out a form. I waited a bit, then swung my bag down and landed it on the desk and said, "Good afternoon. I'm here to visit Mrs. Menotti."

Ms. Stern pushed a register toward me, and I signed in. I signed on a line under a scrawled signature that read 'Henry Menotti.' There was no date. I pushed the register back across the desk. Ms. Stern looked my name over, approved me, and turned to the young nun. "Sister Sarah, could you take this gentleman to the waiting room?" Ms. Stern then reluctantly hoisted herself out of her chair and, with a series of small steps, shuffled down the hall to check on Mrs. Menotti. Sister Sarah broke the ice with a sweet smile, and I followed her into a side room where I was the only visitor. Sister Sarah said, "Please wait here." I settled into a chair and watched Sister Sarah turn on a table lamp and straighten some magazines and start toward the door. Just before she left the room, she turned toward me and I thought she said, "I have to change." She pulled aside the coff, or was it a wimple, shook her head, and her black hair, concealed before and now free, flowed over her shoulders.

A waterfall of black. She kicked off her low-heeled sensible shoes, sending them into the hallway. With a naughty smile she looked at me, put her finger to her lips, marking a secret between us and began to lift the hem of her holy habit and the underskirt. The stockings were a smoky black with seams straight up the back of her legs. She pulled the garment above her knees, and higher, until the white flesh of her upper thigh glistened and lit the room. White, white, skin, untouched by the sun, waiting to be touched by . . . "Mrs. Menotti is ready. You can come now." The Mother Superior motioned from the doorway for me to follow her down the hall and up the stairs.

The room was on the second floor in the back. A large hospital bed was on one side, with tubes, machines, and dials standing beside. Mrs. Menotti wasn't in the bed. She was placed in a wicker chair where she looked out over the ducts and pipes that decorated the roof of the kitchen outside the window. An IV stand was to her side; a tube ran from a bottle of some liquid to her arm beneath the sleeve. Someone had dressed her in a full-length gown decorated with yellow and orange flowers, a robe that, were she not a bit mad already, would have quickly driven her there.

Her warden spoke to her as though she were a five-year-old. "Mrs. Menotti, a gentleman is here to see you. Now sit up straight and say hello."

Mrs. Menotti dismissed the woman with a tiny wave of her hand and settled her eyes on me. She was in her sixties, but her gray eyes, her white hair, her fragile skin were too old for that age. She was trapped inside a body that had betrayed her and she was looking for someone to help her escape.

"Thank you, Mrs. . . ." I said to the stern nun and waited for her to leave.

She did so reluctantly with a parting instruction. "She's not strong, Mr. Harmon, so please, only a few minutes. Sister Sarah will be in shortly to put her back to bed."

Mrs. Menotti's voice was shaky but her manner was direct. "Who are you?"

"A friend of Hank's. I came by to . . ."

"Ah Hanky. Dear Hanky. He was here, you know. He was away for so long, but I knew he'd come. Such a sweet boy."

'Hanky?' That surely didn't help him get through high school. 'Hey Hanky Panky, lend me your hanky.' No wonder he seems bitter. "Yes, a nice fellow," I offered lamely, but Mrs. Menotti was happy to go on, and to talk of her child.

"He looks so different now, but . . . ." Her mind seemed to stop, and she stared out the window. "The birds come; they sit on the pipes." She raised her hand just off her lap and pointed. Another silence, then, "Hanky liked birds. Who are you?"

"A friend of Hank's. I'd like to see him. He was here to visit you. How is he?"

"Here? Was he here? Oh that's nice."

"I wonder if you know where he is." I realized she didn't know, and probably couldn't tell me if she did, but I asked anyway. Maybe there would be something. She looked at me blankly. I tried another tack. "He was a good child, yes?"

"Oh, yes. They both were good. Lovely, lovely . . . ."

"Both?"

"Hanky and Tony. They were so cute. My babies."

"Tony?"

"Hanky was my favorite. Oh, but he could be such a rascal." She smiled. "Boys will be boys. Oh dear." Mrs. Menotti's eyes closed. We sat silently. The home was quiet, just the murmur of the equipment. A low hum of machines, a ticking from something by the bed, some voices down the hall. A red light pulsed from the IV stand; I tried to read the prescription on the bottle.

"Mrs. Menotti," I said softly. "Good morning."

The soft woman's eyes opened slowly. Then her face brightened. "Hanky! You've come to see me. Oh how sweet. Did you bring me something, a present for Mama?"

I opened my bag and pulled out the chocolates, wishing they were gift wrapped, and handed them to her.

"Oh thank you, thank you." She took them and turned the box over and over in her hands. Then her eyes rose back to look at me and a frown slid like a shadow across her face. "Who are you?"

I drove the trip back in the dark, trusting the radio to keep me awake.

16

IT WAS THE SECOND time in a week that LeRoy called—this time it was in the middle of the day and I was lying in bed thinking about getting up. He didn't even start with a good morning. "Blue, Carmen needs to see you. How soon can you get here?"

I sat up. "If I make a cup of coffee, and put on some shoes, say about forty-five minutes."

"Shoes are good but skip the coffee. I don't think she's going to stay here for long."

A half hour later I was standing by the bar, squinting to get used to the lack of light. Inside LeRoy's all optimistic signs of oncoming spring were banished, and I couldn't stay off this case even if I wanted to.

LeRoy greeted me with, "She's really scared, Blue. I haven't ever seen her like this. She's got something and she wants to talk to you."

"Where is she?"

"She's downstairs in the dressing room. She doesn't want to be seen." I turned to go when LeRoy added, "Tell her goodbye for me. Wish her luck—I think she's leaving."

The strip joint was in its afternoon state: a few lights on, chairs upside down on the tables, and the stage in the middle was dark. Behind the stage was a door marked 'Private. No admittance' and 'That Means You.' I pushed open the door and went inside.

I saw my reflection enter the dressing room in a mirror ringed by naked light bulbs. The lights shone over a table with enough creams, ointments, dyes, powders, and lipsticks to keep a drag queen supplied for a year. Carmen was sitting in front of the table, fully dressed with a winter coat and fur hat that tried to hide her body. Her eyes were red, the mascara smeared. Formal greetings were not in order.

"Mr. Heron, sit down. I don't have much time."

I sat down.

She looked at me with doubt in her eyes, then went on. "Billy left me an envelope before he was killed, left it about a week ago. He said to keep it and open it only if something happened to him. I didn't want to open it—I think I didn't want to admit he was dead. Well, earlier today that DA Officer, the creepy one . . . ."

"Officer Weaver, aka Weevil," I prompted. "Yes, I know him."

"Yes. He was asking LeRoy about me, like when I would be here. LeRoy told me. I wondered what Weaver was after so I opened the envelope. There was some money, but something else, some kind of code. Blue, I'm sure if Weaver finds out I have this he'll . . . I don't know what he'll do. I have to get out of here. Billy's gone, and this guy Weaver really scares me."

I heard footsteps on the stairs from the bar. Carmen heard them too.

"Here. Take it." She shoved a business card into my hand. "It was in the envelope. Go see who it is. Now!"

I pushed the card inside my pocket and stepped back through the door. There was a figure silhouetted against the red lights across the strip club floor. A thin shape that looked familiar. I closed the 'No Admittance' door behind me and walked around the stage.

Officer Weaver spoke first. "Well, we meet again. You do get around. Which criminal are you going to help escape this time?"

I could see the answer. Carmen was silently moving across the lounge behind him, moving toward the door to the parking lot in back. She looked at me, a look of desperation, and she slipped out the door.

I wanted to keep Weevil occupied. "You always have the convictions figured out without all that clumsy fair trial mumbo-jumbo. Makes it a lot more efficient, I suppose."

"Don't be a wise-ass, Heron. I didn't come to see you, anyway. Is she here?"

"Try the dressing room. Maybe you'll find someone to shoot," I offered helpfully.

He turned and pushed through the dressing room door. I went to the back door and quickly slipped the bolt and was back in place when Weevil stormed out. He ignored me and ran to the door. It was bolted from the inside. "Did she go upstairs?"

"Who?"

"Fuck!" Weevil charged up the stairs. I slid back the bolt, opened the door, and stepped into the parking lot. A storm was threatening—a churning sky, black clouds, a sense of dread in the air.

Carmen's tail lights turned the corner and receded up the alley. The car didn't hesitate at the red light on the corner—did anybody ever stop for that light?—turned left and sped down Main Street. I started the BMW and followed her path up the alley. Weevil burst out the back door, leapt into his squad car, and started up the alley behind me. I decided to set a precedent and stopped at the corner to wait for the light to turn green. The squad car flashed lights and blasted its siren. I pointed to the red light and lifted my hands, palms up. The loudspeaker in the squad car screamed unintelligibly. The light turned green. I slowly turned left onto Main Street. Weevil's black-and-white squad car screeched off to the right. I watched the back of the driver's head, low in the seat, Weevil's head, covered with short tufts of hair with the mottled surface of his scalp shining through. I recognized that head; it belonged to the driver of the black car that nearly hit me behind the Bistro the night Bill was murdered. The car disappeared down the street with sirens blaring. I smiled; he had turned right, had taken off in the wrong direction. Carmen was gone, and I knew she wasn't coming back.

I drove around the block and pulled over to the curb. Took out the card. William Windsore, President; APOLLO LIGHTING, office address, phone, cell phone, fax, etcetera. Not very interesting. I turned it over. On the back written in pencil, R11—32—13. It reminded me of my high school locker combination. Right 11, Left 32, Right 13; numbers that would reveal secrets hidden away in a locked safe.

17

I WAITED UNTIL THE END of the day to drop by Apollo Lighting. I pulled into the lot as the workers were leaving. The door to the office was unlocked; a small woman was absent-mindedly pushing a vacuum cleaner back and forth across the rug, her head in the clouds. Her mind was on her flowing evening gown as she danced across the ballroom. It was dropping off one shoulder. The eyes of every gentleman in the place were turned toward her. She spun, the dress floating away from her body. She didn't hear me come in. I spotted the large company safe standing conspicuously in the corner. It was six feet high, weighed more than my car, had an imposing set of double combination dials, and there was no way that 11—32—13 was going to convince it to open up and let me in. I left unseen before the dreaming vacuumer finished her dance.

Next stop, Bill Windsore's house. As I drove out of the Apollo lot, the first few drops of rain began splattering on the windshield. By the time I cut behind the Three Bears Bistro to avoid the traffic light, the wind was slapping a sheet of rain on the windows of my Beamer and the wipers were struggling to keep up. Clouds were lowering, bringing on the night before its time.

Bill's driveway was empty. The Mercedes was still parked in the open garage. I took my flashlight from the glove compartment and the nine-millimeter Glock from under the seat, and ran to the protection of the porch roof. I followed the same route I took the night he was murdered. Tried the front door, locked; walked around the deck to the back, staying close to the wall. The wind was blowing off the reservoir, driving rain into the back of the house. The roof wasn't giving me much protection and I was already drenched. It didn't take long to work a credit card on the lock. I let myself in. The flashlight beam played around the living room and paused on the spot on the floor where I found Billy. Police tape outlined a figure who wasn't there. He was in the morgue and the book and the whiskey glass were sitting in a forensic lab.

A flash of lightning lit the room, and the house was rocked by a blast of thunder. A hallway from the living room led to back bedrooms, and Bill's office. It was easy to guess that it was the landscape painting that covered the wall safe—no one ever hid a safe behind abstract art. I fished the business card out of my pocket. Right three turns to clear and then to 11, back to 32. I was jolted by another bolt of lightning and had to begin again. Success. The thick steel door swung open. The flashlight beam lit a sheaf of papers, a few pieces of memorabilia, a watch, a necklace pushed to the back. Another folder packed with Apollo Lighting tax forms. Three 8 × 10 envelopes lay at the bottom.

A shaft of light suddenly streaked across the metal door of the safe. It came from the hallway. Someone had turned on the living room lights and there was no time to get out. I grabbed the three 8 × 10 envelopes, stuffed them under my belt, pulled my coat tightly about me, and closed the door to the safe. I started to work the combination again when the beam of a flashlight hit me. I spun around. The light was in my eyes but I recognized the voice.

"Well, look who's the burglar caught in the act." No raging storm or blinding light could hide Weevil's whine. "Trying to get into the safe, are we?"

I turned my light toward him, lighting up his permanent sneer and the nasty looking pistol pointed at me.

"So Mr. Private Snoop, just what would we be looking for?"

"Thought I'd find a few million, retire early. But it looks like somebody gave me the wrong combination."

"That somebody would be Carmen, wouldn't it. Well I've got a bullet ready to go through that dumb head of yours, so maybe you'd better cough that combination up. Maybe it'll work for me."

"You're welcome to try." I shifted my flashlight beam to aim at Weevil's eyes, stuffed the business card in my coat and replaced it in my hand with the Glock. "You're not going to take me in—quit bluffing. You're looking for something your boss sent you to find. What might that be? Maybe Billy-Boy had something on Peck? Maybe that would be something that Peck wouldn't want in the open? Maybe that something might be in this little safe?"

"Maybe you could get shot for breaking and entering," Weevil hissed back. "Maybe I came to check on the house, you pulled your gun, and I had to shoot you. Maybe you should get off your high horse and start explaining why you're here." Weevil lowered his pistol and blasted a bullet into the floor by my feet, scattering oak parquet splinters across the room.

This was turning into a war of nerves; two guys with guns, both partially blinded, trying to get the upper hand. Not a pretty sight. I kept talking. "Maybe you want to get in that safe, maybe I want to get in that safe, and maybe it just ain't going to happen until the boys in blue get in that safe." I turned my pistol slightly and blew away a floor lamp. The shade slapped into the wall, glass shards flew from the shattered bulb, and the frayed wire short-circuited with a burst of sparks. Fuses blew. The hallway went dark.

"You fucking asshole! You can't bluff me!" Weevil moved his pistol a few inches and fired. The picture window behind me blew out with a deafening crash. A shower of glass flew out toward the Lake, and the storm leapt inside. Rain began pounding on my back; wind scattered paper around the room.

We stood facing each other. It was a standoff. A bolt of lightning hit the Lake, the blast of thunder shook the room, and the phone on the desk jingled from the electrical charge. Weevil swung his pistol to the side and blasted the phone off the table. I brought my flashlight down hard, hit his and both lights went out and I heard his pistol hit the soaked carpet. The room was pitch black. Weevil crashed into something, and I ducked out the door into the hallway.

I felt my way to the living room and backed against the wall. Another bolt of lightning scorched the room with white light just as Weevil's head came through the door. It was a good target. I brought the solid butt of my Glock down. The thunder clap covered the sound of a body hitting the floor.

By the time I started the Beamer I was dripping wet and shaking. I stepped on the gas and left a bucket of gravel on Bill's front porch and spun on to Reservoir Drive. The light was red at the corner, so I cut through the Three Bears' lot, nearly hit a couple who were running through the rain for their car, and turned on to 131. I'd be gone before Weevil could wake up and get to his car. He wanted what he thought was in that safe, but the combination was in my pocket and the contents stuffed into my belt.

18

THE RAIN HAD LOST its violence and settled in to a steady downpour. The thunder and lightning had moved on. A few flashes lit clouds in the distance. It was late and Ralph's Pizza, not far from the Arms and open until two, was my last chance for food. I pushed open the glass door and left a trail of puddles up to the counter. My favorite waitress wasn't there.

"Where's the gossamer gal?" I asked the young woman behind the counter. "Haven't seen her for a while."

"She'll be back tomorrow. Took a week off to go home, see her folks. You just made it. We're about to close."

"That's what she always said."

"You know her?"

"We were in love."

"News to me."

"News to her too, I suspect. It was unrequited."

"Is that like unrequested?"

"She used to throw me out after two, although she did give me the option of screwing her on the salad bar."

"And?"

"Never did."

"Sorry, no chance with me. See you tomorrow?"

"Maybe."

I ran next door for a six-pack of Boston Dark Ale and was looking forward to a quiet dinner alone. I turned the radio to WRCK to keep up my spirits, and headed down Machinist's Drive. The Apollo Lighting buildings were dark now, maybe in deference to the death of the owners. The only lights left on were in the ground floor office. The parking lot was a sea, and streams of water flowed down the side into the graveyard. Who was going to run the business now? Neither Bill nor Jason had a wife or kids or heirs as far as I knew. Looks like our town is in for darker nights and fewer red traffic lights to run.

Tonight, I was glad to be home in the warmth of my apartment, safe from the rain that drummed on the fire escape, washing off the soot from the asphalt plant and cleansing the evil spirits from the air. Safe for the moment from DA Peck and his handymen, I stripped, toweled myself dry, and found some clean jeans and a cozy red flannel shirt. I opened the pizza box, opened a bottle of the Dark Ale, and opened one of the 8 × 10 envelopes.

The envelope was crammed with copies of deeds, bank agreements, and mortgage papers. I'm no financial expert, but it was easy to see that Billy's empire was in deep debt. Papers detailing double mortgages on the business and the houses and letters threatening foreclosure. Seemed like every bank in the country owned a piece of Apollo Lighting. I stuffed the financial mess back into the envelope and sat back, finished off another beer and a slice. Billy was in financial trouble. Did he owe money to someone who got tired of waiting? Killing the guy who borrowed it is not usually the best way to get a debt repaid.

I opened the second envelope. It was full of letters, letters written by Bill and folded in envelopes. I skimmed through a few of them. They were scrawled in longhand and laced with swear words, hate, threats, and accusations. The letters told a history of abuse and hate, all wrapped up neatly in envelopes addressed to his father, envelopes that were never mailed. I found only one letter to Bill from his father dated a few weeks before the father was murdered. I unfolded it and skimmed through. It read like a letter one would write to an accountant, or a lawyer. It was typed on Apollo stationery, business-like and official. He wrote that he had had an affair a long time ago and now he wanted to help his illegitimate kid, that he was going to rewrite his will. The letter was as cold as ice. Bill's letters were sheer poetry compared to this. The father was oblivious to the son's feelings, and the son was incapable of confronting the father. A bomb waiting to explode.

I replaced the letters in the large envelope and opened the third. A series of photographs slid out onto the table. I had them spread them in a row and was trying to make sense of them when the Valkeries in my cell phone saddled up to ride again. My grandfather used to sing "Look out for the car tracks!" to the tune of the "Ride of the Valkeries." Ruined my appreciation of Wagner forever.

"Blue? Is that you?"

It was too late for JJ to be calling, unless he had to be back on the job. "Why aren't you home with the family, JJ? You should try getting fired—frees up a lot of time."

JJ's reply was serious. "I'm back at Bill Windsore's house, or what was his house. Up in smoke. A pretty spectacular blaze."

"It burned down?"

"It went up too fast to be an accident."

I was suddenly worried that the Weevil could have been lying where I left him when it burned. "Anything left— anything to sift through?" I asked.

"There's nothing but rubble. The firemen got there in time to be pretty sure no one was inside, but they couldn't do much. They could still smell the gasoline."

If Weevil wasn't cooked, he probably was the one doing the cooking. "Sounds like someone wanted to make sure something was not found."

"Sure does." JJ said suggestively. "Any ideas what that might be?"

"Yes I do. Can you meet me at the diner tomorrow morning? I've got something you'll want to see."

"Okay, but one other thing, Blue." JJ's tone was suspicious. "You might wonder why I'm calling you so late. A couple leaving the Three Bears earlier this evening was nearly run over by a silver BMW with a dented hood, going like a bat out of hell. Now who do think that could be?"

"Not a clue, JJ. See you tomorrow morning, around ten." I snapped the cell shut, and slid the photos back into the manila envelope.

19

A T TEN O'CLOCK IN THE morning, the One-O-Clock Diner had already served most of the responsible customers and sent them off to work. The ten-o'clockers were more difficult to categorize, parents having a late breakfast after dropping the kids off at school and guys sitting alone in booths trying to eat off a hangover. I greeted the waitress, who tilted her head toward the back. I asked her to bring a cup of coffee. JJ was waiting for me in a booth as far from the door as possible. He was gazing at a bacon burger and a plate of fries with eager anticipation.

"Good morning, JJ. Is that breakfast?" I slid into the booth.

JJ bushed aside the comment with a wave of his fork. "Jesus, Blue, I feel like I should be wearing a disguise. If anybody at the precinct saw me with you . . . ." He left the thought unfinished.

"A bit of an overreaction, don't you think?"

"Blue, I mean, you helped a suspected murderer escape, then sat back while a homicide takes place on the other side of your apartment wall, and now you're spotted fleeing from a building that somebody, I say it, set on fire. For chrissake! You want me to give you a gold star?"

The coffee arrived and I poured in real milk and real sugar, a gourmet treat compared to my usual. "It doesn't look so good, but I can explain. First, JJ, tell me: did your crew get anywhere with Eddie's murder after you sent me to my room?"

"First off it's not Eddie. It's Jason Windsore."

"Right. Jason Windsore." I dutifully repeated.

"One thirty-eight-caliber bullet, close range. He must have been asleep or . . ."

"Or in an alcoholic daze." I cut in. "That's his normal late-night state."

"As for the investigation, you've got quite a group of neighbors. I think I could have found a reason to lock up every one of them."

"We're just one big happy family."

JJ ignored me. "Do you think a bunch of hookers is going to give you a straight answer? The only one we could trust was that librarian chick, but she slept through the whole thing. All we could come up with was that there were a shitload of johns in your building that night. Your neighbor Stella Starlight had a guy there, but from what you told us, he was humping away on the other side of the wall when Jason was shot. She didn't give us much of a description; said she would look at a line-up if necessary. But given the parts of him that she described in detail, it would have to be a line-up of naked guys."

"Not much to go on," I added helpfully and reached over to steal a fry. "But it seems to me that Jason would have to know the guy before he opened his door and let him in that late at night, but that's not for sure."

"Or the perp had a key. As you said, Jason was probably out of it—I doubt he could get up to open a door. We pulled the bullet out of the wall. It went right through the poor guy's head—I doubt he felt anything. You're lucky it didn't keep going through the wall; it was headed your way."

"Any prints—fingerprints, footprints, fibers, DNA, RNA? You know—all that stuff that solves your cases for you?"

JJ scowled. "This ain't TV, Blue. We have to do the footwork. Now, what have you got, and it better be good."

I handed JJ the envelope.

JJ munched on his burger and took his time looking carefully at each of the twelve pictures. "Strange. They're a bit fuzzy, but that's DA Peck, all right."

I described the photos. "Twelve pictures, each at the same angle. Two people sitting side by side in the front seat of a car. And the time printed on each—all after midnight."

"Peck is in the driver's seat in every picture. Who are the girls?"

"I recognize some from LeRoy's club. A couple are dancers. The rest I don't know."

JJ studied the pictures. "The blonde looks pretty young—and this one too."

"I'd say jailbait."

"Our District Attorney. Our happily married family man, our defender of moral rectitude, our Sunday-church-going-protector-of-our-morals, our District Attorney with a bevy of young floozies, some a bit too young. This stuff is dynamite. Where did you get these?"

"Carmen, one of LeRoy's strippers. She's the one who had an affair going with Bill Windsore. He left a sealed envelope with her a few days ago and said if anything happened to him, open it. Something happened to him, like getting killed, and she did. There was some cash, and a business card with a bunch of numbers on the back. Peck apparently got suspicious, and sent Weevil to see her, scare her, shoot her. Something like that."

"Carmen gave the card to you?"

"She realized the DA was sending his thugs around. With Bill gone, she's got no insurance. She got scared. Gave the card to me and flew the coop. I prevented Weevil from going after her."

"Blue! You got in the way of a cop again?" JJ sighed. "Could you for once let the law do its job? And how are you going to explain this to the Chief?"

"Trust me on this one, JJ. There's no way Weevil's going to report that. And I'm sure we won't see Carmen again. She's smart enough to put a lot of miles between herself and this town. No reason for the DA to go after her either—it would just open up a hornet's nest."

"Go on. The pictures?"

I handed JJ the business card. He looked at it, then turned it over. "What do you think?" he asked.

"The numbers looked like the combination to a safe, so I checked the Apollo office. They have a safe but it's as big as a truck, requires a lot more than three numbers to open. So I went over to Bill's house and let myself in."

"Broke in, most likely."

"Found the safe in his office, behind a painting, of course. Combination worked. The photos were in the safe."

"Okay. So then you burned down Billy's house?"

"No." I laughed. JJ didn't. "I had a visitor. Weaver turned up and we played a round of Russian Roulette. I tricked him into thinking the pictures were still in the safe, gave him a bump on the head, and got away with the goods. Weaver didn't have the combination, so he followed Peck's instructions to get rid of the blackmail material. I suspect he burnt the house down, trying to roast whatever was in the safe."

JJ pondered the photographs. "These are strange photos. Don't know what to make of them. Where did these things come from?" JJ wondered.

"I don't know yet, but what I do know is that the DA is out to squash anything and anybody related to these photos. So now we have a guy who wanted to get rid of Billy Windsore, and who had just the thug to do it. And," I added, "I saw him leave the area the night of the murder."

"Great." JJ groaned. "Now I suppose you think I should go arrest a cop. Well, not yet. A motive is not the same as some kind of proof." JJ dug back into his fries with a vengeance.

I gulped down the rest of the coffee and picked up the pile of photos. "Maybe I'd best hang on to these for a bit, give you some breathing room."

JJ gave a wave of the hand, which meant he was happy not to have them. "All right. By the way, Kathy gave me something for you; seems she still believes in you. It's a bit of background on the dancers. She went by LeRoy's. He wasn't eager to let the stuff out, but she mentioned getting a warrant and he gave her what he had. There's not much there." JJ dug around in his pocket and pulled out a crumpled piece of paper.

I took the sheet, flattened it, folded it, and slid it into my shirt pocket. "JJ, next Christmas I'm buying you a briefcase." I stood up to leave.

"Just a second, Blue. How did Weaver know you were going to Bill's house last night? Did he follow you?"

"That would have been pretty hard. When I started he had taken off in the opposite direction. He was after the blackmail photographs, and after he saw me with Carmen, he must have guessed she told me something. Went to Bill's, I suppose, to case out the house."

"He would have done that already, as soon as he could after Bill died." JJ had a point, as he usually did. He always thought of things that I should already have thought of. He went on. "And Weaver turned up when you went to the Windsore house to find Hank?"

"Yes."

"And he walked in today when you were with Carmen."

"The guy must be clairvoyant."

JJ kept on. "I know ESP, witchcraft, and psychics can explain everything, but . . ."

"Just a minute, JJ. I see what you're driving at. Wait here."

"I'm not going anywhere until I finish my lunch," JJ said, his mouth full of burger.

I left the diner and went to the Beamer. I reached inside the wheel well on the passenger side and slid my hand from front to back. Nothing. I walked around to the other side and repeated the motion inside the left front wheel well. I felt what I was looking for, knelt down and pulled it off the chassis. "Aha!" I announced triumphantly and held up a square box about the size of a cigarette lighter. JJ gave me a thumbs up sign through the window. GPS with a magnet. My Beamer was a pretty blip on somebody's computer screen.

So Weevil's been tracking me from his car. Or getting someone back at the station to track me and calling the info to him. I took the device and looked around the lot until I saw a car with Florida plates. I reached under the fender and stuck the GPS on. The Weevil needs a vacation—a little time on the beach will do him good.

20

I LEFT JJ TO SNEAK back into his office—tainted by his association with me. I'd helped Hank Menotti—the prime suspect in two murders—escape. I'd let an important witness disappear. I hadn't told JJ about the scratch on Hank's car. I felt that Hank needed to be protected from the DA's hit men. Something told me that Hank wasn't and never had been a murderer.

I hadn't recognized that Eddie Jones was Jason Windsore. Hard to explain to normal folk that this was consistent with the culture of The Gold Hill Arms. There was a reason that people chose to live in a building at the end of an industrial wasteland, next to a graveyard. It was anonymity, a desire understood by the frequenters of The Arms—that's why we unofficially renamed it The Dung Hill Arms. Eddie's mailbox said Eddie Jones. We knew it wasn't Jones—it was apparent that Eddie was running away from something. None of us wanted to know what it was. To do so would have meant looking too closely into a mirror.

The detour sign was still there, so I took the long way home and parked by the side of the Arms. I greeted Javier in the lobby, a man who was able to manage a building and look the other way at the same time. I picked up a copy of the free local paper and checked the mail. One letter stood out from the usual. I never liked official mail. My first thought is always "They found me out!" The letter was from the traffic department. Inside, a ticket for running a red light. Are they serious? How are they going to pin that on me? I pulled out a photograph. Damn it, look at that! A snapshot of my car running the light when I left the lot behind LeRoy's, with date, time, and location. There must be a camera at the intersection of Main, Cedar and the alley by LeRoy's. Enclosed was a nice photograph of my BMW. You could read the license number, see the dent in the hood, and count the rust spots. At the top of the picture, you could see that I needed a haircut. A quick call on my cell and I was on my way back to the center of town. I had to talk with Annabel Lente.

I couldn't find the maintenance guy, but I managed to make it through the basement maze on my own. I pushed open the door to the Traffic Division. The techies were busy in their subterranean game room; they were doing a lively business collecting fines. Annabel Lente was at the far end of the room. Her back was toward me as she bent over a console to help one of her brood. I waited by the door until she stood and noticed me. She was truly a creature of the underground, tall and thin with gray hair, a black dress, and white skin that seemed never to have seen the sun. We met in the center of the room. I asked her if we could talk in private and she took me into the darkroom. She closed the door behind us. She wasn't wearing sneakers.

"What's up, Mr Heron?" She was not aware of my pariah status.

I handed her the ticket. "Got this in the mail today."

Annabel studied it for a moment, then, "I can get rid of this if you'd like."

"Is it that easy to fix?"

"Sure. For cops, and weren't you working for the force when you ran that light? Cops are always on a mission or a chase or something. Any summons they get, we disregard."

"Just another perk for the men in blue."

"For the police, and for the Mayor, the DA, the Comptroller, and a whole stack of official guys."

"What do you think of this?" I handed her one of the pictures that I'd pulled from Bill's safe.

"Wow!" was all that Annabel could say. "That comes from a traffic photo. A bit of cutting, Photoshop, sharpen it up and enlarge and this is what you get. The District Attorney, isn't it?"

"Why wouldn't he have jumped on these?"

"He never would have gotten them. I'm sure he runs red lights all the time and never even thinks about it. He never sees any tickets."

"And he wouldn't expect a camera to be pointed down an alley in any case. I think these are all taken coming out of LeRoy's back lot."

"The camera there is to cover the intersection of Main and Cedar, but when they put in cameras they usually aim them in all four directions. These pictures were taken at night. As I remember, that camera was one of the first to go in, and they lit the corner up nice and bright to make sure the license would show up at night."

"Who would have seen the pictures after they were taken?"

"There are a few people in the office here who could see them. Other than that, we keep it pretty tight. We really don't want publicity when it comes to which public figure gets a pass to go through red lights."

"Can you bring these images up on the computer?"

"No way. They're wiped off the computer as soon as we pull them. And some of these look pretty old too. None of these would show up, unless, of course, the Apollo people kept them on their computers."

"The Apollo people?"

"Apollo Lighting. They install, monitor, and repair the cameras, and they have a pretty extensive computer system to keep track of it all."

"And that system was run by Billy Windsore, wasn't it?"

Annabel could see what I was driving at. "Is this blackmail? A couple of those girls look pretty young!"

"Best not get involved just yet, Miss Lente. You may have to explain to the chief how this works, but until that happens you probably shouldn't mention it."

I thanked Annabel and worked my way up to the surface, making only a couple of wrong turns along the way. Back on the street I let my eyes adjust to the daylight, then picked up a coffee from the cart at the corner and settled into my park bench. This bench was becoming my office. A quiet spot for reflection.

I sat back, streched my legs, and decided to watch the sun set behind the corner of the courthouse. It was the end of the workday; a stream of figure flowed out of the offices around the park, and with few goodbyes, scattered off in all directions. Cars filled out of the parking lot behind LeRoy's. They stopped at the light, then turned the corner on the way to the suburbs. They were driven by civilians who probably had received a surprise summons in the mail and were hunbled into obeying the red signal. An hour passed; the sidewalks emptied. The few cars driving down the street turned on their headlights, and I thought about Bill Windsore.

He had run across one of the pictures on the Apollo equipment. He could see the possibilities for blackmail, and no doubt searched for other photos. He found twelve, and cut, cropped, and sharpened them up. Twelve times DA Peck had picked up a late-night date—a stripper, a prostitute, a young girl—and take her somewhere. Twelve times he drove though the red light on LeRoy's corner. Twelve times he put his career on the line. Twelve times DA Thurmond Peck had posed for a family portrait.

21

I STOPPED AT THE LIGHT, waiting to turn on to the North end of Machinist's Drive. Given the irrelevance of the old factory district, I figured the road would be repaired in a year or two. The streets were deserted—not unusual for the evening in this part of town—and I was thinking of Billy, and Jason, and the whole dead Windsore clan when the light turned green. I didn't move but stared at the light. It turned yellow, then red, as traffic lights do. I sat there: green again, yellow, red . . . Bill was thinking of the blackmail— thinking that he used the traffic photos to blackmail DA Peck. The DA wanted those pictures. Was he telling me that when he was dying? Traffic lights, blackmail, motive? Red, green, yellow, red, green . . .

The guy who had pulled up behind me began leaning on the horn. I waited for the next green and made the turn. About one hundred yards down the Drive my cell rang. I slowed down, opened the phone, and was greeted with a distraught voice.

"Heron? Is that you?" It was a bad connection.

"Who's this?"

"Hank Menotti. Come meet me?" It was more a command than a question.

"You name it. When and where?"

"Now. Soon. At the old Warren Furniture place on Machinist's Drive. It's close by your apartment, just next to Apollo Lighting. I'll be there in half an hour." He spoke quickly, and his voice was breaking up over the phone.

"I know where it is."

I was about to flick the phone shut but Hank wasn't finished. "Heron. One more thing. Nobody else. Just don't bring anyone, or I'm gone. Got that?"

"You're calling the shots, Hank. Hope you know what you're doing."

The phone went dead and I stepped on the gas. I thought it would be a good idea to get there before Hank. Five minutes later I pulled into the deserted parking lot of the now dark and abandoned Warren Furniture Factory. The Glock was hidden under the front seat—I pulled it out and stuffed it in a side pocket. I left the BMW on one side of the lot and walked by piles of rusted bed springs to the other side. I hid behind the shed at the side of the factory and waited for Hank to appear. There was only one hitch to my plan, and that was the gun barrel that was pushed into my spine.

"Don't move! Keep quiet!" I recognized Hank's nervous voice. I turned. He was holding a small flat silver semi-automatic. A powerful little gun that could be easily carried and could very well be 38-caliber. He held out his hand and

I gave him the Glock. "And just what were you planning to do with this?" he hissed in my ear as he pushed it into his coat pocket. "Let's go around back." He pushed me ahead of him with the gun and steered me along a path by the factory wall.

"In there," Hank ordered. I pushed the door to what was once the factory's sales office. It was unlocked and opened with a groan, turning on one good hinge. Hank lit a candle, a sad light that barely reached the wall, and pointed to a wooden chair. I blew off a thick layer of dust and sat down. He stood in front of me holding the pistol in his shaking hand, alternately pointing it at me and the floor. He wasn't comfortable pointing a gun at anybody, but he wanted me to know that he was in charge. I saw no reason to challenge that.

"Okay, Heron, I don't want trouble. I'm in enough already. But there's a couple of things I have to say."

I tested the back of the chair. It held. I leaned back and stretched out my legs. Anything to try to relax Hank. "You're calling the shots. I'm listening."

"I should thank you for the other day—but I might have been better off in jail even if they did beat the shit out of me."

I laughed, trying to lighten the mood. "It didn't do me any good either. The law thinks I planned your escape."

Hank wasn't listening to me; he had something on his mind. "It was me that night in the parking lot. I was there. That scratch? You clipped the bumper of my rental car." Hank couldn't stand still. He began pacing back and forth across the room.

"I know."

"But I didn't kill Bill Windsore. I considered it. I mean, I had enough reason to kill the son-of-a-bitch. Guy kills my father, gets me framed for twelve years in the jug. Gets all the money. Yeah, there's plenty of reason, but I didn't do it. I didn't even go in. I didn't have the nerve."

"Who then?"

"How about Peck? Rumor has it that Bill was blackmailing him." Hank was barely hanging on to his composure. I still hadn't gotten used to staring down the barrels of loaded pistols, especially since the folks at the other end tended to be deranged. I've found from experience that the very existence of a lethal weapon in a man's hand badly distorts his perception of reality.

"You think Peck killed Bill? Why do you figure?"

"No, he'd send somebody. Probably that Weaver asshole."

"You're right about one thing: Bill was blackmailing the DA."

"With what?"

"Affairs with prostitutes. A couple of them under age."

"That explains a lot—doesn't surprise me. But why are you telling me this?" Hank was pointing his finger in my face. I wasn't sure he realized that it wasn't his finger; it was the pistol.

I answered quietly, "So you might feel better about telling your story to the authorities? I'll get you in safely."

"No way, Heron. I was at the scene of the crime. I got all kinds of motives. I probably would have killed him if I'd had the chance. That's probably why they decided to go after him now. I was stupid enough to come back, and they see a patsy.

A chance to bump off Windsore and set me up once again."
A breeze blew through the broken windows, and the candle
went out. Hank cursed in the dark. I waited while he found a
match and lit the candle again. It wouldn't have been hard to
push Hank into doing something stupid, like shooting wildly
in the blackness. I followed my rules of engagement with a
loose cannon—the three D's: distract, deceive, delay. "Hank,
where's your brother these days? Tell me, where's Tony?"

"My brother? What . . . Tony?" Hank looked perplexed,
and then the faintest smile crossed his face. "Oh him.
Haven't seen him in years. You know where he is, good, but
I don't give a shit."

"Just asking. So what are you going to do now? You'll
get pulled in sooner or later. You can't hide forever. You
know that."

"That's where you come in, Heron. I'm figuring you
can do something with this info. Get me off the hook, then
I'll come in." Hank had a strange way of asking for favors.

"I'll do what I can. No promises. There's not much to
go on, and I'm not in much of a position to challenge Peck."

Hank looked confused, unsure. A man without a plan.
He lowered the pistol. "Wait here until I'm gone."

There was a crash when the remaining hinge snapped
and the door fell to the floor. The candle went out. A second
crash was my Glock coming through the one window that
still had some glass in it. A car started behind the factory,
lights swung by the open door, and I spotted the Glock and
picked it up. Hank turned out of the parking lot and on to
the Drive—his back wheels sent a shower of gravel against
the factory wall.

Five minutes later I'm parked beside the van sunk into the mud at the side of the Arms. Five more minutes I'm leaning back in my easy chair, martini in hand, feet on the window sill, gazing into the night. The moon was three quarters full, and the railroad yards twinkled as though the departing rain clouds had dropped a light shower of diamonds on the land. In the bright light of day the secret of the diamonds would be revealed as shards of broken glass, plastic bottles, and bits of tinfoil left by hundreds of careless hands. The sad whistle of the three-o'clock express floated over the yard, and I waited for the headlight to come into distant view. The express track ran across the far end of the railroad yard, far away enough to assure anonymity for the faces in the windows. Those who couldn't doze off peered over the deserted yards and thought of where they were going, or where they had left. I wondered if any of them, someone with a lively imagination, could imagine me, leaning back in the easy chair, feet on the window sill, martini in hand, watching them rush by. Passengers in express trains, trains that wouldn't even stop in our town, left me both envious of their future and fearful of death. Fortunately I could always look up to the sky. The infinite lessons held in the language of the universe—black holes, parsecs, and figures like ten million light years—brushed away all silly concepts of life and death, good and evil, and all the metaphysical shudders that would pop out of a closet in the mind just when you're trying to make a good impression on a pretty Chief of Police.

I remembered the crinkled sheet of paper that Kathy had sent me via JJ. I found it in my shirt pocket, and rubbed it flat on the window sill. It was the background information Kathy had dug up about the dancers. Kathy started off with a disclaimer written across the top of the page. *Blue—this isn't much, just some preliminary stuff I got, mostly from LeRoy. Chances are much of it is made up.*

Dee Dee Darling, aka Marie Rosalie del Toro. 26 years old. Grew up in NYC. Kathy had written in the margin: *DD's parents are still in NYC—(I can probably find them if necessary). She left home, dropped out of college after a year, and has been kicking around clubs since then, mostly in Boston.*

Stella Starlight, aka Bella Antonia Garibaldi. Age unknown. Has been dancing for a number of years. Gave her previous address as 895 West 53rd Street, Manhattan. (Don't believe it—that address doesn't exist.) Arrived at LeRoy's about 2 months ago.

Carmen, aka Gretchen Soznikesky (or something like that). Age about 35 (she's the senior citizen on the staff). Émigré from Hungary only about 2 or 3 years ago. (I doubt her papers are legit.) Has been with LeRoy since she arrived.

Not much there, but . . . Carmen is gone. Dee Dee doesn't seem to be involved. I need to talk with Stella. Tomorrow night after she gets home, I'll stop by. That means I have an appointment at about three in the morning.

22

MY BRIEF VACATION IN dreamland was interrupted by a buzzing—a creature was scampering around the table—some bug looking for crumbs, or, my cell phone. The calling number suggested that somebody at the Town Hall wanted to say good morning. I obliged. "Good morning. Heron here."

It was DA Peck's office, telling me to come in. I didn't recognize the voice, an Eastern European accent. Maybe Kozimov.

"How about tomorrow morning?"

"Not possible. The District Attorney is speaking at a conference tomorrow. Come in today, later, after work, about six. He'll be free then."

I was beginning to feel like the main suspect in this case, or as the law prefers, the perp who's called in to testify and cannot refuse. I wasn't going to go unarmed. I selected one of the photos, one with a particularly young-looking girl sitting a bit too close to Mr. Peck in the front set of his car, folded it carefully, and slipped it into my breast pocket.

It was a bit after six and the court house had emptied for the day. Strangely, there wasn't anyone at the downstairs desk. I made my way unnoticed to Peck's realm on the third floor. Dumpling was at the desk. He didn't smile and I sensed a look of pity. I guess he knew that when he ushered poor souls into the inner office, Peck was going to pass judgment on their sins—or at least on those sins that Weevil and Dumpling had encouraged them to confess to. "You can go in."

The DA aimed his black eyes at me and started firing verbal daggers before I got through the door. "Heron, what the hell do you think you're doing? You've managed to interfere with a serious murder investigation, you helped a chief suspect escape, you let another killing occur right under your nose, you prevented us from talking to a possible witness, and it looks like you broke into a house for some goddamn reason and then burned it down." The DA looked like Robert E. Lee working up a justification to keep the battle going a few more days so he could ride in on a white horse. He forgot, however, that when Lee did that, it was to prepare the scene for his surrender. I thought I'd let him strut a bit before returning the fire.

"Look, Heron, these are criminal acts. I haven't decided what to charge you with or how much time you'll spend behind bars. I'm a fair man, Mr. Heron, and I'll give you a chance to convince me otherwise. Just what can you offer me in return?"

A voice in the back of my head was shouting at me, but I didn't hear it. "Will this do?" I said, and held out the photograph.

DA Peck looked at me, and didn't move or react. I started to take it back when he reached out and snatched it from my hand. Stared at it for a minute and dropped it on his desk. "What the hell do you mean by this, Heron?"

"What do you think?" I wasn't sure where this was going, but I was pushing Peck to slip up and give me something.

"Blackmail? Are you seriously thinking of blackmailing your way out of this? You have one out-of-focus picture of me and a woman riding in a car, and you think it means something?"

"Blackmail, yes. But not me. You know that. How much have you been paying Windsore to keep this out of the news?"

"Where did you get this piece of nothing?"

"That's a good question. Maybe you should ask Officer Weaver. Seems he's been trying real hard to get his hands on this."

"You're on dangerous ground here, Heron. Are you sure you're big enough for this?"

"Here's the problem, Mr. Peck. You're a District Attorney and it should interest you. The person who was blackmailed would have a good motive for getting rid of the blackmailer. When Hank Menotti shows up you see an easy mark to pin another murder on. After all, you're experienced at this—stuck the charge on him twelve years ago. A pretty flimsy case, but you wanted a nice news story to help get you elected. Prosecutor solves gory murder case, sends murdering son to prison. It worked. A last-minute jump in your numbers and you squeaked into the DA's office. Now maybe you could try that again, get rid of Bill Windsore, and send Hank back for another stint—a nice long one this time."

"There's nothing here, Heron. One picture, in a car. Nothing happening. Do you think it means anything?"

"I've got eleven more of them and the time of day on each, or I should say the time of night. I'm sure we could run some of these gals down. A couple of them are dancing at LeRoy's right now. And if we trace the ones who are still too young to be dancing there, you've got jailbait on your hands. Seems to me the question here is whether you'd like this to get to the press—you seem to like being District Attorney."

"You are so full of shit, Heron! First off, I did Menotti a favor twelve years ago. I let him plead guilty to manslaughter. I could have hit him with first-degree and put him away for life. And do you really think I'd sneak over to Windsore's house and stick a knife in his back? I suppose I also walked by your apartment, busted in on your neighbor and blew him away. Are you friggin crazy? No jury is going to buy that! Just what do you want?" Peck fired the words at me with so much anger that his mustache kept flapping up and down after he finished.

I stubbornly kept going, "You don't do things yourself, Peck. You get others to do your dirty work. Let's talk about Officer Weaver."

"What about him?"

"He was there the night of the murder, in back of the Three Bears." The shouter in the back of my brain was getting louder, but I had ignored it for too long already.

Peck glared at me. "What are you after? You say blackmail isn't your thing. And I don't figure you're trying to get me fired so you can be the next DA." Peck stopped, then pointed a threatening finger. "You have a lot to lose here, Heron, believe me, a lot more to lose than you seem to be aware of. I'm asking you again, and for the last time: What do you want out of this?"

"I want to know who killed the Windsore brothers, that's all. And I don't want to see Hank Menotti framed again." I stood up to leave. "You can keep the photo. Frame it and show it to your wife and family." I turned to find Officer Weaver standing in the door, holding that damn pistol again. I was sure he'd reloaded it by now, but I wasn't so sure he wouldn't shoot me this time.

"You can sit down again, Heron." Peck's voice took on a different tone, quiet, efficient, and menacing. He stood and walked to the door. "He's all yours, Weaver. He knows you killed Windsore so you'd better figure out a way to keep him quiet. There's no one here—just make it clean. After that take him out the back stairs. Kozimov will give you a hand." Peck didn't look at me, I was already erased from his memory. He closed the door behind him.

The voice in the back of my brain quit yelling at me, and just said "You stupid fuck!"

Weevil sat himself into Peck's leather chair with apparent pleasure. I was hoping he'd lean back and put his feet on the desk. No luck, he leaned forward and lay his gun-carrying hand on the desk with the barrel pointed at my Adam's apple, and grinned at me. At least I think he grinned. The sneer side of his mouth turned into a grin, but the grin side turned down into a sneer. It was late. The room was still, the building was empty, and the street was quiet. There was no one left in the world except me and Weevil.

"So you know I killed Billy?" Weevil's eyes shifted nervously between me and the pistol.

"No, I don't. I just know that you were there that night." I put off asking him if he enjoyed his vacation in the sun.

Weaver scowled at me. "You told Peck you knew I killed him."

"No, I didn't. I said you were there. I showed him a picture and it got him all riled up."

"Ah yes, the pictures." Weevil became almost chatty. "I never got to see them. Are they good?"

"Very pretty. Nice for the family photo album." I tried a different tack. "If I remember right, it was Peck who told me you killed Billy. Just a few minutes ago."

Weevil cursed. "That prick! He'd sell me down the drain just to save his parking space."

"Officer Weaver," I started, "we should talk about . . ."

"Shuddup!" Weevil spat. I became aware of a clock ticking somewhere and a car alarm that sounded up from the street below. The world was starting up again but without me. I wondered how long it would be before I was missed. I thought about how long it would take for the milk in the fridge to turn sour. I thought about Kathy. I thought about how stupid I was to show Peck the picture. I tried not to think about Kathy.

Weevil broke the silence. "I didn't kill Windsore." He sat back in the chair.

I said nothing.

"I was going to. It was worth a lot to Peck, and he was willing to give me a wad of bills to do the dirty work. I was there that night. I was going to see Windsore and try to talk him out of those pictures, out of the whole blackmail thing. Threaten him, I don't know. But I couldn't kill him. If I was any good at killing people, you wouldn't be here today."

I had to agree with that.

"Anyway, I never made it. I recognized Hank's blue rental parked behind the diner, and I was getting out of there when you came busting around the corner." Weevil spewed out a series of grunts that sounded like a stuttering pig. I think he was laughing.

"If that's true, how come Peck tells me you killed him?"

"Cause I told Peck I killed him and I got a nice paycheck. Easiest money I ever made, and how's he supposed to know?" Weevil laughed again.

"That explains why Peck wanted me off the case. He had ordered a murder, thought he could keep an eye on the Police Department, but I was a loose cannon." I wanted to keep talking, as the alternatives didn't look too good. "So who do you think killed Bill? You think Hank did it?"

"Sure. Why not? He had all the motives."

I relaxed a bit. "Why'd you burn the house down?"

"Thought the photos were still in the safe, but you got 'em, didn't you."

I nodded. I didn't want to rub it in.

"Showing them to Peck was pretty dumb. You must have some kind of death wish. What were you planning on?"

"I don't know," I said honestly. "I was hoping Peck would throw some light on the issue. Pretty dumb, you're right." It's a good idea to flatter the guy who's holding the gun.

Weevil's response surprised me. "Personally I don't give a shit what you do with the pics. Got nothing to do with me."

"What are you going to do with me?" I asked as flippantly as I could, trying to ignore the pistol.

Weevil stood up—took the gun off the desk and shoved it back in the holster. "Guess you got the upper hand and escaped."

"And Peck?"

"He won't like it, not one bit. But what's he gonna do. I know a lot more than you do. As long as he thinks I bumped off Windsore I get to keep my nest egg. And because I can testify he told me to kill him, and because I know about the pictures, he'll leave me alone. You go find who killed Bill Windsore. Just leave me out of it."

Weevil left the desk reluctantly. He probably didn't get much chance to sit there and pretend to be the boss. "Stay here a few minutes, then go out the back stairs. I'll turn off the alarm." There was that grin again. He walked out of the office, through the reception room and into the hallway, leaving the doors open behind him. Kozimov got up from the reception desk and followed. The Weevil had just passed up another opportunity to shoot me.

Evening at The Arms. It was important tonight that I repeat my ritual of easy chair, feet on the sill, martini, and daydreaming over the tracks and stars. The business meeting with Peck had left me marveling at my own stupidity, or was it the mirage of immortality, or naiveté, or possibly just a simple death wish. That's all good psychoanalysis, but the explanation that stuck was just simple stupidity. I gazed at the sky and drew the summer triangle with my eyes— Vega to Altair to Deneb, the faintest of the three. It's taken fourteen hundred years for that light to reach me. That should put a little perspective on the matter. I've got some time to think about it; Stella won't be home before three. Damn, somebody drank my martini—better get another.

23

THREE IN THE MORNING, I'd heard the door to 3B open and close and knew Stella Starlight was home. I stood in the hallway wondering how I was going to approach the exotic stripper. I would try to keep a professional manner, but some other options raised by the visit didn't seem so bad. I pressed the buzzer. An innocuous 'ding-dong' sounded inside, designed to mislead an innocent visitor about the siren he was about to meet. She opened the door. I doubted that the usual wear for a police interrogation was a gauzy red slip that ended not far below her waist, just low enough to make the concept of her sitting down an intriguing idea. Stella Starlight had breasts that showed off the extent of modern technology; her slip was no match for their prominence.

She expected me. "Come in, Blue. I was hoping you'd drop by."

The living room was comfortable and traditional, with a décor that reminded me of visits to my great aunt: a large soft flowery sofa facing a coffee table, standing lamps with gold-fringed shades, a warm throw rug, and paintings featuring hills, valleys, skies and waterfalls in ornate frames.

"Please sit down." Stella turned the dead bolt on the door and motioned toward the couch. I obliged. "Would you like something?" she asked, without explaining what the something might entail. She sat next to me.

I took a note pad from my jacket, and a pencil, and began: "Miss Starlight, let me just ask a few simple questions. Bill Windsore is dead. You knew him from LeRoy's. When did you last see him?"

Stella smiled at my formality and gave me a straightforward answer. "Last week, Sunday, I think. Yes, Bill was in the bar. He wanted Carmen and me to leave with him but we had to dance downstairs. He'd had a few—that wasn't unusual—and left in a bit of a huff."

"Did you see him often?"

"I know what you're getting at, Blue, but I'm not going to talk to you about business. You can understand that, I'm sure."

Then, it hit me: "Okay. Fair enough, Toni. How about Henry Menotti? How do you know him?"

"You mean the guy who killed his father? No, I don't know him. Why would I want to know him?"

"Maybe, Toni, you've known him for a long time."

"Enough inquisition, Blue. Let's . . . ." The word froze on Stella's lips. Then, with an anger that was quick to rise, "What's this 'Toni' stuff? What are you saying?"

"Toni, Antonia Menotti, Hank's sister. You've missed him while he's been in jail."

Tears came to Stella's dark blue eyes; her emotions were in overdrive. She waited for me to go on.

"That's why you were at the funeral. It was the funeral of your father."

Stella gazed at the floor and into the past. "I never knew him. I came to say goodbye." She said it so softly I had to bend toward her to hear. She shifted closer to me on the couch and put a hand on my leg.

"That must have been hard." She was crying; I reached over and touched her cheek. "And to lose Hank, your brother, to a long run behind bars."

"Yes, we're brother and sister. We're twins actually. We grew up without a father, without money, barely with a home. We had each other; we *are* each other. We loved each other from the day we were born." Stella paused, choked back a sob, then went on. "We found out that our father was alive when he called Hank and wanted to see him. Hank went to meet him and they took him away from me for twelve years. I've waited until now for him to be free." Stella regained her composure, and her hand slid up my leg.

"Do you ever see your mother?"

"No," she said firmly. "She doesn't like me, never did. I don't really know why; maybe I reminded her of herself." She lifted her eyes from the floor, and searched mine like a child who looks to her mother for help. At the same time, she was unzipping my fly and I could feel the interview part of this meeting slipping away.

I tried once more. "Why come back here? Why now?"

Stella shifted her knees. A glimpse of black hair reminded me of the woman in the funeral picture when she was still Toni. Now she is Stella, the red-haired stripper protecting her brother, and she had decided that the Q-and-A stuff was over. She bent down to kiss the head of my cock, which had been lured out of the unzipped fly into her hand. Her tongue slid around the tip, and I couldn't think of any further questions.

"Come," she said, and not letting go she led me into the bedroom. I was trying to imagine how to strip for a stripper but she took care of the undressing. She was more skilled at taking off clothes than I was, and soon she had me lying naked on my back on her king-sized bed, surrounded by enough pillows to supply a good sized harem. Stella Starlight was demonstrating her skill at fellatio, while I marveled at the red-flowered wallpaper. It rose from a red rug, traveled across the ceiling behind a large overhead fan, and down the opposite wall. We were in her workshop now, the laboratory, the tool room, the place where she conducted business. Two large bureaus stood along one wall and two closet doors were closed—one could only guess at the paraphernalia that waited inside. I rolled her over and pulled down the straps of the slip. Lying on her back had no effect on the size of her breasts, but more startling were the studs piercing each nipple. Barbells, with crystal globes hugging each nipple from both sides. With my pointing finger, I traced a line from one nipple to the other, then down to another jewel in her belly button, and then farther, along a trimmed vertical path of black hair, to studs decorating a pair of generous lips. I was at the source of Stella's financial security.

"That's a lot of metal," I observed.

"Has to be big enough to be seen by the audience," Stella explained. "But it can be embarrassing at the airport," she added with an innocent twinkle in her eye. She reached to a drawer by the bed and brought out a condom. "Just for good measure." She wasn't Toni any more.

I watched as she rolled it on with admirable expertise, and then I slid inside her. She was as wet as a New York City curb during a rainstorm. Well, at least she likes me, but then she is a professional. Can a good prostitute turn on the flow, just turn on the spigot, or can she convince herself that she really wants the guy, that he is the best she's had? A nice idea until I remembered reading in the *Science Times* that a woman can be wet when raped. A Darwinian safety valve to minimize the damage.

"You thinking of your stock portfolio, big guy?"

"Just hoping you're having a good time."

"Of course I am. I've felt some large cocks in my day, but yours . . ."

Stella had practiced her lines well and of course I believed her. She was good at the trade, she was working now, and for a moment, she was distant; then her body began to betray her. Toni had returned. She reached with both hands to the back of my head and held me, looked into my eyes, pulled my lips to hers. I felt her quiver as our tongues touched. She pushed her fingers through my hair and began to cover my face with kisses. I pushed slowly, deeply, into her and held myself there, stationary, unmoving, letting the anticipation, the desire for rhythm overwhelm us. Toni pushed against me. I kissed her forehead.

Stella fought her body, her alter-ego, and regained her professional poise. "Watch. I can liven it up a bit." She reached to her breasts, to the barbells that penetrated the nipples, placed a thumb and forefinger on either side of the crystal edges, and pressed. Lights, action—the glass globes on either side of the nipples began to flash. Red and yellow on the left breast, red and green on the right. Her large globes were writing a symphony in lights. They were playing out her act, *The Music of the Spheres*. The lights on her breasts pulsed, sometimes in sync, then drifting apart like the independent windshield wipers on a commuter bus. *Red ... red ... yellow ... green ... red ...* I began to slide in and out. Stella responded and we were dancing around the hall; we dipped, we swooped, we bent and twirled and followed the music, and the bed began banging into the wall, the other side of my wall, with a beat that was all too familiar. I tried to follow the rhythm of the lights: *red ... in ... red ... yellow ... out ... green ... red ... red ... in ...*

"Like them? They work well on stage," Stella purred, and took over the lead in the dance. Her body moved in perfect harmony with the flashing lights. I followed. I was the pole in her act. We moved as one, together.

I was staring at the blinking lights. I was hypnotized. Good for making love, I thought. These lights are hypnotic. They paralyze your lover, they paralyze the victim. Victim? Why did I think victim? Flying saucer my ass! Traffic lights my ass! "You killed him!" I blurted out, surprising myself more than Stella.

"What?" She continued to answer my thrusts with her hips. Her skin was soft and wet and slippery. Her body was warm. Her body was hot, burning hot. Her hands were everywhere, on my back, on my shoulders, and around to my chest, pushing me away and pulling me in with the same motion. She couldn't hear me.

"You!" I was beginning to yell. "Killed him!"

"No, I . . . ! No, No!" Stella cried, and she clutched at me. Her arms surrounded me and she held on with every ounce of her strength. I could barely breathe.

I whispered, whispered into her ear. "Toni, you killed him. I know this. You mesmerized him, you held him, you pulled him to you and you stabbed him in the back. You . . . you . . . ." I had to catch my breath.

Stella's body tightened. "Oh God!" She was on the edge. I was on the edge.

"Stella, you killed him," I whispered again and bit her earlobe. I felt a spasm rise from her toes, through her legs, into her sex, across her stomach, over the flashing breasts and to her brain, to her mouth. "Yes!" She cried. "Yes, I killed him! I stabbed him, I murdered him, I . . . ." She shook with a sexual peak, a sexual revelation, and I came inside her. We were one, the accuser and the accused, the hunter and the hunted.

We lay still now, holding tightly to each other, intertwined. The right breast flickered and went out. Dead battery, dead man. The left breast kept up a lonely pulsing; red . . . yellow . . . red . . . yellow . . . . She was warm and shaking as though with a low fever. I was soft and hidden inside her, somewhere in the wet folds of her body, and neither of us wanted to let go.

Minutes passed, hours passed, days passed, and I slid out of her and rolled over. We lay on our backs side by side. The ceiling fan spun slowly, sending reflected red and yellow flashes scattering around the room. A flake of red paint broke off and dropped toward us, winking in colors on the way down. "They're supposed to paint every couple of years," I said.

"I'll talk to Javier," Sylvia said quietly. Then, "Billy Windsore deserved it."

"I know," I said. "I know."

The room was quiet, a cooling breeze came through the open window and the fan spun slowly overhead. Toni spoke first. "What will you do?"

"Take you in. What else can I do?"

She already knew that answer. "You won't hurt Hank?" she pleaded. "I wanted to do it together but he's too soft-hearted. I took his car, I was there alone. I didn't even tell him what I'd done. He doesn't know. You have to believe me. It wasn't Hank."

"What about Eddie? Someone shot him. Maybe that was Hank? He's still got the pistol. You were fucking away on the other side of my wall when Eddie was done in. And I do remember that the guy had some pretty terrific staying power; my pictures were falling off the wall."

Stella laughed, a dry humorless laugh. "You private eyes are all the same. Pin it all on sex. My bed was bumping against your wall, yes. But I wasn't in it. I went by your window, stopped for a moment to watch you having fun, then climbed in Jason's window. He was in a drunken stupor.

I shot him. Put him out of his misery. I was out the door and back in my apartment before you even moved. You told the police that I was fucking—you were part of my alibi."

"Your bed can fuck itself?"

"My bed's none of your business." She wasn't going to explain. "Blue, you can do whatever you want with me. I don't care. But not yet. I'm not done." Stella rolled quickly to her left, grabbing for the open drawer on the night stand. I rolled at the same time and we both reached for the pistol. She started to claw, scratch, and bite. We rolled off the bed and crashed to the floor. I landed on top holding her hand. Her hand was holding a silver semi-automatic. It looked familiar. With a twist of the wrist I had the gun, but my bare skin was losing the rest of the battle to her nails. I pushed her flat to the floor, sat up and pressed the barrel of the gun into her ribs. She quit fighting and lay still, breathing heavily. She guessed my thoughts. "Yes, Hank borrowed it for a bit. But he didn't use it—it wasn't even loaded."

I started to rise, holding the gun in position. Her left breast kept blinking at me.

"Sorry, Blue," she apologized. "Nothing personal."

I didn't know what she meant, but Stella was looking beyond me, and I should have seen it coming. An explosion in my brain. Flashing stars replaced the flashing crystals.

I thought I landed on top of Stella, but that wasn't where I found myself. I opened just one eye. The pillow looked familiar except it was covered in blood. Jesus my head hurt. My pillow, my bed. I'm naked but in my room, in my bed, in my pool of blood. Movement was too painful. I decided not to try to open the other eye, but just wait it out, and I faded out again. The world was very quiet when I tried again. The clock read four-thirty or something. I was cold. The window was wide open. Maybe if I could concentrate I could get up to close it. On the floor now, crawling to the window. Try to stand. Now, just pull it down. It's cold. Get a blanket from the bed—rather bloody blanket. I felt the left side of my head. Shit, it felt like a meteor crater. I sat in my chair, pulled the blanket around me and decided, or someone decided for me, to wait for morning, to sleep and to dream. It was a Technicolor dream . . . *red* . . . *green* . . . *red* . . . *yellow* . . . *red* . . . *black*.

24

A SOFT HAND WAS ON my cheek—a cold towel on my head. "Blue, are you there? Speak. Say something. You've got me worried."

I opened an eye, and closed it against the bright sun. "What time is it?"

"Ten-thirty."

"In the morning?"

"Yes, you dummy. In the morning. That's why the sun is up."

I opened the other eye. There was Kathy, adding a new compress to my head. "What are you doing here? How'd you get in?" I slurred.

"Through the window. It seems to be the main route in and out of your place. I came by to check the Jason crime scene. Thought I'd say hello and knocked on your door. Your car is outside and I was pretty sure you were home, but there was no answer. I got worried and came in from the fire escape."

Waking up to Kathy brought back wonderful memories, but the throbbing in my head drove them away.

"What happened, Blue? You took quite a blow." Kathy tenderly stroked my cheek. "Looks like a blunt instrument. Drew a lot of blood—there's some on the window sill and on the floor—but the wound's not deep."

"It was next door, Kathy. Stella lives there. I was interviewing her."

"Without your pants? Are you trying to combine the good-cop, bad-cop interview all in one?"

"It was an in-depth interview. One thing led to another." My thoughts were still pretty foggy. Kathy didn't take her hand from my cheek. She waited for me to continue. "She did it, you know. She killed Billy, and she killed Eddie."

"What are you talking about?"

"She blinked her lights and confessed. She killed them both."

"She blinked her lights? And she was so impressed with your love-making that she just flat out told you her life story?"

"She did it, Kathy. She killed Billy! She killed . . . ."

"I think you've made that clear. Mind filling in some details, like what kind of lights are you talking about? You are not making a whole lot of sense."

"She didn't confess at first. But once she turned on the lights, they started blinking. Her breasts, they flash. They had me in a trance, but I figured it out. She used the lights to put Billy so off guard she could wrap her arms around him and put the knife in his back. They're hypnotic, really."

Kathy looked at me like I was a bit crazy. "Have you ever seen a pair of breasts that didn't put you in a trance?"

I tried to make some sense. "It's her act, *The Music of the Spheres*. She's got these lights on her nipples, see. And they blink on and off with this crazy rhythm. Like red, green, red, yellow, green. Understand?"

"No. But do go on."

"I told Stella that I knew everything. She didn't deny it. In fact I think she was rather proud of it. She hated Bill. He killed her father and framed her brother and sent him to the state pen."

"Her brother?"

"She's Antonia, she's Toni. She's Hank's twin sister. They are twins. Really. Like Gemini, the evil twin and the good twin."

"Okay, enough with the astrology. So, Stella gets her revenge, you figure out the lights, and she confesses everything. So why do I find you all bloody and in some kind of mental fuzz?"

"Someone clobbered me. We were fighting over a pistol and then, whammo!"

"And then you were dragged back here?"

"Must have been. Let's go next door. We can go through the windows." I grabbed Kathy's arm and pulled myself out of the chair.

Kathy watched me trying to steady myself, then offered helpfully, "You might put on some pants before you start climbing in and out of windows."

"Yes. Good idea. Where?" I slowly took a step, then another, squinted to bring the room into focus, and found my pants and shirt folded nicely on the kitchen table.

"Stella won't be there. I'm sure of that." We climbed out my window and on to the fire escape. I was still unsteady, but managed to slide Stella's window open and climb into her apartment. Kathy followed, steadying me with a strong hand on my back. Everything was neat and in order. There was no blood to be seen, no Stella to be seen.

Kathy gave the apartment a quick professional search. She checked the closets. "Clothes and suitcases seem to be here—doesn't look like she's left town." We went into the bedroom. "Nice wallpaper. Must help move things along." Kathy patted the bed. "This is where she hit you?"

"No, actually we were on the floor."

"Okay. I won't ask why you were screwing on the floor. How did she hit you?"

"Stella didn't. Someone came from behind. I was pretty sure we were alone. The door was locked from the inside." I was about to explain more when, still a bit dizzy, I stumbled and stubbed my bare toe. "Ouch! Damn it!" A flat edge of metal peeked out from under the bed.

Kathy took out a handkerchief—always the professional—reached under the bed, and drew out a square heavy object. "It's a bookend, a heavy bronze bookend." Kathy held it up to the lump on my head. "Right here. A solid blow." She studied the weapon. "I wonder where this came from. They usually come in pairs and I don't see its companion. In fact there isn't a book in this entire apartment."

My befuddled brain began to come into focus. "I got smacked on the left side of my head from the back with a bookend in an apartment with no books by someone who couldn't get in. Like maybe by a left-handed librarian who's in love with Stella and lives next door with a window on the same fire escape."

"Whatever you say, Blue. I'm trying to follow."

"Come on." We climbed back on to the fire escape, and forced Sylvia's window open. No one was home. The apartment was neat, very orderly, and full of books. A table by the window held a row of books which had fallen to one side, missing the support of one of their bookends. The remaining bookend was solid bronze, a lovely art deco design, a perfect match to the one we found under Stella's bed and to the pattern printed on the back of my head.

I was thinking out loud, "There was no john that night. Sylvia was the one who kept the bed banging against the wall and gave Stella an alibi while she sneaked over and wasted Eddie."

"You're still not making much sense, Blue. I'll chalk it up to the bump on the head. But tell me again, why do think Stella was wiping these guys out?"

"I don't think it. Damn it, I know it! Revenge is the tale. Revenge. Stella and Hank are twins. Stella, aka Toni, turns up here and gets a job at LeRoy's only a couple of months before Hank gets out of prison. She meets Billy at the club, and I suppose she moved in here to keep an eye on Jason."

"Wouldn't Bill recognize her?" Kathy wanted to get every detail filled in.

"He'd never seen her and wouldn't recognize her. When Hank got out of prison, they were going to kill the Windsore brothers."

"They did it together, the twins, Hank and Stella, or Toni?"

"No. Hank didn't have revenge in his soul. He's kind of a pussycat. He puts on a good show, but he wouldn't hurt anyone. He fought with Stella at LeRoy's that night, tried to talk her out of it, but it didn't work. She told him she was just going to scare Bill. She left alone, but she took his keys and his rental car. She was alone when she stabbed Bill."

"And Hank?"

"Now he realizes what she did and wants to save her. He tried to convince me that he drove the rental car over to the Three Bears' lot that night but denied killing Billy. The twins love each other; he'll do anything to help her. Even take the rap again."

Kathy was turning this over in her mind. "And Sylvia was head over heels in love with Stella, enough to become an accessory. You can fill me in later—like some more on the Music of the Spheres stuff—but right now I think we'd better concentrate on finding this pair."

"Wait!" Stella's last words before I went blank were coming back to me. "Not yet. I'm not done," I repeated mechanically.

"What's that?" Kathy asked. "You still seem a bit out of it."

"'You can do what you want with me, but first I have one more thing to do.' Stella said that just before I was whacked."

"One more thing to do?" Kathy was worried "Sounds like one more *person* to do and that doesn't sound good. Who else was responsible for taking Hank away from her?"

"Peck!" we said simultaneously.

Kathy saw the danger immediately. "Let's get to his office. Just in case."

I remembered what Peck's secretary's had said: "He'll be at the conference center. He's presenting something to the press this morning."

"That's upstairs from the library. Sylvia has no reason to believe that she's wanted. I wouldn't be surprised if we find her at work."

Kathy was worried now. "We'd better get moving." Kathy started out the window. She paused for a second with one leg over the sill and looked me straight in the eye. The strip of non-regulation pink that winked at me made me realize that the bookend hadn't caused any permanent damage to my mind. Kathy smiled mischievously, swung the other leg out and stood on the fire escape. I followed, and we climbed back into my apartment. I finished dressing as quickly as my unsteady body would allow, and we rushed downstairs.

"We'll take my squad car," Kathy said. "You're not in any shape to drive."

Kathy backed out, and put the pedal to the floor. I sat in the suicide seat. My head throbbed. When we turned on to the highway, the flashing lights came on and the siren wailed. I doubted we would get there in time.

25

W E SLID TO A stop in front of the Library and left the squad car perched halfway up the curb. Policemen, reporters, and onlookers were milling about. It was clear that an important person was holding forth in the conference room upstairs. We avoided the crush at the conference center door and took the left-hand door directly to the Library. Inside, the books looked over a strange oasis of quiet. Sylvia was at her desk, concentrating on her mail, doing her best to hide from the world around her. A cup of coffee and a croissant sat untouched to the side. Kathy was right—Sylvia was trying to act as normal as possible, assuming no one knew she had whacked me on the head. Stella had convinced her to go to work as though it was just another workday morning. She didn't look up when I stood in front of the desk.

"Good morning, Sylvia."

She saw me and visibly jumped. "Blue?" Her voice betrayed her—she was far from becoming a hardened criminal.

"Tell me, Sylvia. Where's Stella?"

"What? Who? I don't know." She stuttered.

"Where's Stella? Don't waste my time!"

"Blue, I don't know what you're . . ."

I swept my arm across her desk, sending papers, books, the coffee and croissant scattering across the floor. "Don't fuck with me, Sylvia! Where's Stella?"

The unnerved librarian's eyes filled with tears. "Upstairs, she's upstairs. In the conference room. No, maybe in the side room. On the third floor." She pointed to the back stairs. "Don't hurt her, Blue. Please don't hurt her." She began sobbing. The five patrons of the library sat with their books open in front of them, watching in stunned silence.

Kathy and I moved quickly. Through the fire door to the back stairs; double time up the two flights to the third floor hallway. I could hear Sylvia running up the stairs behind us. Two doors on the right were to the lavatories, then a janitor's closet. One unmarked door on the left and farther down an open double door with a few people standing outside in the hall listening to the proceedings. Sylvia came through the door from the fire stairs and pointed to the unmarked door on the left.

The first person we saw when we entered the room was Officer Weaver standing flat up against the back wall with his hands in front of him as though he was holding someone off. Opposite him was the door to the conference room, and Hank Menotti was standing next to it. I could hear a loud lecturing voice on the other side of the door—DA Peck's commandeering style was recognizable. Along the far side of the room was a wall of windows, with a glass door leading to a terrace. Stella Starlight was standing in front of the door holding the small silver pistol with two hands. It was pointed at Weaver's chest. She swung it toward us.

"What are you doing here? Don't get in the way! This slime has it coming to him." Weaver's hand started to drop toward his holster. Stella swung her pistol back, aimed at his chest. "You toad! You deserve to rot in hell!"

"I didn't . . ." The Weevil sputtered, raising his hands to the ceiling.

"Quiet!" ordered Stella. "Blue, get out! And take your girlfriend with you. This doesn't have anything to do with you." She turned the gun back toward Weaver. Kathy was not going to take that comment too well, and I knew that given one trace of a chance, she'd be spraying Stella with a hail of lead.

Hank pleaded with Stella: "Toni, don't. It's not worth it. Let's just get out of here."

Stella straightened her arms, aiming the pistol at Weaver. "He beat you up, Hank. He pushed you into confessing. He needs to die."

I stepped in front of Weaver.

"What are you doing? Get away!" Stella's hands were shaking.

"Not him." I did my best to speak calmly. "He may be a slime-ball, but he didn't put Hank in the pen. He didn't frame him. He didn't kill anybody."

"He's Peck's goon. Get away, Blue, or fuck it, I'll shoot you, too."

"Makes him a rotten Boy Scout, but you can't kill him for that."

The room was frozen into a tableau, a scene in a staged melodrama. Stella Starlight, the star, the driving force, the producer and director, was center stage. Her small but deadly pistol held straight out in front of her with two hands, pointing toward Weaver. Weaver, frozen, back to the wall, shaking, his arms held high in surrender. I'm standing between them, the fly in the ointment, holding up the action, questioning the plot. Kathy, poised, her right hand tensed beside her, ready to strike, a deadly force focused on Stella's every move, waiting for the right moment. Hank and Sylvia, helpless, terrified, saddened beyond hope, unaware of their roles, each with a love for Stella that had unknowingly given fuel to her hatred.

A burst of applause came from next door, followed by the sound of chairs shifting, shuffling feet and voices. The door from the conference room flew open and DA Peck appeared, a group of conferees at his heels. Stella turned toward him, kept her pistol straight out in front of her, and with no hesitation fired two rounds into his chest. Peck crashed into the door frame, blocking the crowd and the shouts and cries behind him. Screams came from the conference room as the audience pushed and shoved their way out the door and down the hallway. The Dumpling appeared behind Peck and was trying to pull him out of danger. It looked as though he was dragging a sack of cement.

Stella had swung the pistol back toward us. Kathy had moved closer to me. Her hand was on her pistol, which was halfway out of the holster. I stayed in front of Weaver. Hank had frozen in place like a cold marble statue in a museum. Sylvia stood in the doorway, sobbing. Stella turned and pushed the terrace door open. Kathy's pistol was out in a flash, but I reached over and pushed the barrel down.

The sound of the terrace door slamming shut and the snap from Stella's pistol were simultaneous. Blood splattered on the outside of the glass, leaving patterns like pressed flowers in a young girl's diary. Sylvia's screams filled the room. Hank didn't move. Weaver pushed me aside and headed for the bloody terrace door.

I looked at Sylvia. She cried out hysterically. "Blue, I'm sorry. I didn't mean for this . . . I'm sorry."

"Quiet!" I ordered. "You didn't do anything! It was Stella who put this rut in my skull. You weren't even there!"

Hank crossed the room and folded Sylvia into his arms. He held her as though he was holding his beloved sister, Toni. Toni who would do anything to avenge Hank, to get revenge for the years in jail that took him away from her. Sylvia held Hank as though she were holding her lover, Stella, the force in her life that she could not resist. Weaver pushed the terrace door open and stepped out.

A group of the curious was pushing to get through the door from the conference room. People react to a murder either by running away in fear or by running toward it with curiosity. Weaver came back into the room from the terrace. He looked at me and shook his head, a thumbs down. Stella was dead. Then he gave me one of his smiles. I think it was a smile. Maybe he was thanking me. We were even; neither of us had killed the other. He crossed to the hall door and began clearing the crowd to make space for the army of police and medical teams that were about to arrive. Kathy was bending over Peck, taking his pulse. She looked over at me and shook her head. The post of District Attorney was up for grabs. She punched buttons on her cell phone, held it to her ear, and began issuing instructions to the sirens that wailed from the street below.

I put my arm around the Sylvia-Hank figure and pushed them toward the door. I steered them down the fire stairs. I wanted them out of there before the reporters began with the questions. We went down the two flights and back through the fire door into the Library. It was empty. A real shooting will take precedence over any mystery novel, and the readers had left to join the crowd of curious onlookers outside. Sylvia, in a daze, cleared the books and papers off the floor. Hank carefully mopped up the coffee with a paper towel. I told them what to do. "Hank, take Sylvia home. Then go down to the precinct and tell them everything you know about Stella. Ask for Inspector JJ Cakes. I'll tell him you're coming."

"What about Sylvia? What should I say?" Hank pleaded.

"Just leave her out of it."

Sylvia was about to speak; I stopped her. "Go. Go out the back. Don't be part of this media circus. Just stay out of this." I pointed to the door, like the Lord ordering Adam and Eve out of Paradise. They left out the back, held together only by their loss.

They were guilty. Sylvia knew Stella killed Bill, but she wasn't part of it. So did Hank. They were both trying to protect her after the fact. They both loved her; they were blinded by that love. All the stars of this drama were dead now: Bill, Jason, Peck, and finally Stella, Stella who used to be Toni until hatred consumed her. Sylvia and Hank were bit players, actors who had some lines, but the plot went on without them. In the real world the small fry get caught and take the rap, and the big guys go free. This time we got it right. Bill killed his father; he's dead. Jason helped; he's dead. Peck thought he had Bill killed; he's gone. Antonia, Toni, aka Stella Starlight, played judge, jury, and executioner. She wrote and starred in the last act, and she's dead.

I stepped out into the sunlight and pulled the front door of the Library closed behind me. The lock clicked shut; the sound had a finality to it like the closing of a book that you've finished reading. I found Kathy's cruiser and leaned against it to wait for her. It would be a while, but I wanted to see her and I had nothing better to do and I couldn't think of anywhere else I wanted to be. I'll watch for a while, watch the world go churning by. Watch the ambulance crew roll out the stretchers and run them inside, hoping to find a heartbeat. Watch the police cars multiply, filling the horizon with an array of blinking, blinding lights. Watch the eager reporters with their telescopic lenses run up to try to catch someone in an unguarded moment. Watch the curious crowds press forward and the officers in blue hold them back, all wishing they were upstairs gathering grisly tales they could tell for years to come. I tried to analyze the patterns, to make sense of them. I copied the diagrams they made on the ground into my mind, searching for the geometry in the movements. Scientists find patterns everywhere and use them to explain where we came from and why we're here. The old astronomers found patterns in the sky, patterns in the movement of the planets. They drew the orbits, first in circles, then in ellipses. And in the patterns they found music, *Music of the Spheres.* I'll stand on the sidelines and wait, and observe, and listen. I want to hear the music.